Uncle Wonderful

By Edward J Funk

Copyright © 2019 Edward Joseph Funk. Registration # TXu 2-167-825

ISBN# ISBN-13: 978-1-7320732-1-0

This book is available in print at most online retailers.

Table of Contents

Table of Contents 2

Chapter 1: Ambivalence 3

Chapter 2: Sleazebag...24

Chapter 3: Battle with No Winners...............................42

Chapter 4: Cowboy Ty...58

Chapter 5: Second Strike 73

Chapter 6: Michael...90

Chapter 7: Jake the Lover 109

Chapter 8: Emotional Lockdown 128

Chapter 9: Frank's Special Place 147

Chapter 10: Journey into Darkness 167

Chapter 11: Encounter 187

Chapter 12: Released 205

Epilogue: 223

Studio City, California, 2006

Chapter 1: Ambivalence

Jake's six-foot frame was sprawled on the oversized burgundy faux leather couch, which was much too large for the small living room of their bungalow. A sofa pillow edged his thick, blonde, wavy, hair. His gray blue eyes, almost the color of slate, were directed toward the television. He was watching a Dodgers baseball game that marginally held his interest.

His wife, Maddy, was curled up a few feet away in a matching chair. Maddy also had held onto her childhood blondeness, aided by some strategic streaking here and there. Her long legs were beneath her. Maddy tanned better than Jake and her copper-colored skin, along with perfect cheekbones, accentuated the jade color of her eyes. She was reading the Sunday paper, the early edition one could pick up at the market on Saturday. She commented, "Did you see the

Book Section in the Times? There's a Frank Ford book reviewed."

"What do they say?"

Maddy didn't know if Jake was in the mood to hear anything about his uncle but it wasn't her nature to tiptoe on eggshells. When she had something to say, she said it. Still, she was relieved that he seemed open to something about Frank Ford. She had been trying to get Jake to contact his uncle, his only family in Southern California, since they had moved west the previous January.

She stated, "He's written a book about the scion of a San Francisco banking family, and this reviewer wasn't terribly impressed. Quote: 'Frank Ford has once again written a biography that tells you everything about a subject except what you want to know.' Apparently, he skims over the juicy stuff."

Jake responded, "I don't think he's ever had a best seller but he must sell well enough. At least you see his name in airport bookstores from time to time."

"Was he older or younger than your dad?"

"A few years older," Jake stated flatly and then paused. Maddy knew what was coming. "I know what you're up to," he said critically. "This is as subtle as you get. It's a prelude to your pressuring me to go visit him. I should have seen it coming." Jake turned his head and held his look, waiting for a response.

Maddy met his eyes without flinching. "I don't know why you think that my every word to you is some kind of calculation. You should know me better by now."

"That's just it; I do know you better." A new coldness had wafted into Jake's voice.

Maddy could be equally frigid. "There's another one of your opened-ended comments, not really saying anything, just biting."

"Okay, I'll point out some of your calculations. We now live in Southern California where you grew up. Specifically, in the San Fernando Valley, twenty minutes from your mom. Our daughter is being groomed to be a replica of you. It's just all happening this way."

Maddy was surprisingly caught off guard. There was truth in Jake's accusations. She had hoped her dreams would become their dreams; she had thought, given enough time they would. Maddy tried keeping the tears from welling in her eyes. She started to mutter something, but her voice was too soft, too vulnerable. She stopped and left the room.

She didn't stalk out. It was her very effort to regain her composure, regain her dignity, that cut through Jake. He had gone too far. Jake knew how to go on the offense. He had learned from the best. Jake heard a door shut, the Dutch door in the kitchen that led to the drive, the door that Maddy loved when they first saw the house. Then there was a start of an engine that faded as it rolled out the drive and headed west down the street. Looking at the clock, he guessed that Emily's dance lesson would be over soon.

Jake suddenly felt very alone and not just because he was by himself. He had spent much of his life alone and was used to it. He had hurt Maddy. Maddy had an honesty that sometimes scared him. But, her love, too, was honest, and he had never known anything so intoxicating. Now he was feeling raw and it was his default setting to steer clear from painful feelings. He had learned that at a very young age. Instead, he focused on survival. In an instant, he knew what he could do. He turned off the TV, went into the bedroom, and unearthed a piece of paper stuck in the pocket of his golf bag. Written on it was an address and phone number.

Jake was fairly sure he knew where Frank Ford lived. While still living in Chicago, his best friend Jonathon sold software, mainly to large law firms that provided proprietary information on just about anyone in the world. No unlisted number was sacred, no real estate transaction left unrevealed. He asked Jake for a name to research. After more than a few beers, a flash in

Jake's head conjured up the name of Frank Ford. Jonathon had him on the screen in an instant.

Jake had ambivalent feelings about Frank Ford. No, they were more angry than ambivalent. He remembered him when he was a kid and he had been crazy about him. It seemed like his uncle came often from California to visit. Uncle Frank didn't treat him as some sub-species to adult humans. Rather, he treated him as just a younger person, deserving equal respect. Uncle Frank was willing to help him with whatever project he was undertaking. And another thing: he was playful in what he said, expecting a child to have a sense of humor. And Jake did, maybe more then than now.

Tom was Jake's father's name. He died of cancer when Jake was six. He was only thirty-five, a brilliant civil engineer. He had been brilliant to Jake as well. Jake would remember a particular afternoon when he was probably no older than four. He was looking out his bedroom window, watching his father get out of the car to come into the house. It was a sunny day, and the sun played off of his blonde hair as he walked around the back of the car. Jake felt good just seeing him. There was a kindness, a gentleness, that Jake saw on his father's face. And Jake imagined that everyone else saw the same thing.

A few years later, Tom became weak. Jake didn't know that his dad was dying until he was dead. Then he saw him laid out at the funeral home. He touched his cold stone hand and knew what it meant to be dead: gone, never to come back. He saw it on the faces of all the adults who tried to smile when they looked down at him. Their fearful eyes betrayed their smiles and Jake found the dichotomy disturbing.

His mom was the only one who seemed herself. Karen Ford had a matter of fact way about her, at least the Karen Ford most people knew. And now more than ever, that strength was admired. Everyone knew that she would get through this, no worry about that. She'd forge ahead and be able to take care of herself and her son. It was even hard to think of her as a widow, just two days after Tom's death; her getting on with life was so certain. What a blessing for the boy.

Uncle Frank attended the funeral. He and Tom had looked very much alike, even for brothers. Both had blonde hair and blue eyes, although Tom's eyes had been a deeper blue, like the sky that day when Jake had studied his dad from his bedroom window. It was only at the funeral home that Jake took notice of the resemblance and was comforted by it. He wasn't capable of taking a good look at himself and realizing that he'd grow up looking just like one or the other.

Uncle Frank had been the most distraught of the mourners. In the same way he had always treated Jake as a full, thinking human being when he played with him, he didn't try hiding his pain from Jake now. At the cemetery, when it was finally over and time to go, Frank had picked Jake up and held him tight. Although he wasn't crying out loud, Jake could feel the heaving of Frank's chest and he knew he was crying inside. It was as if Jake was given permission to cry out himself, and he did. Jake sobbed and Frank cried aloud, too, and everyone seemed to walk away a little faster. Karen stood by, discomfited. For once in her life, she didn't quite know what to do. That day had been the last time Jake had seen his Uncle Frank. He had gone back to California and disappeared from his life.

Now it was twenty-three years later and Jake stared at the piece of paper with his uncle's address and phone number. A feeling rushed over him, almost like an ache, he so fiercely wanted to see his uncle again. But just as quick, anger rose. Why had Uncle Frank abandoned him when he had needed him the most? His dad was gone in what had seemed like an instant; it had taken longer to realize that Frank wasn't coming back. What kind of man could have done that to him? He had asked his mother about Frank, and her answer, in so many words, was always the same: expect nothing from him and that's exactly what you'll get. In time, he knew it was best not to ask.

Jake felt the anger he had known as a child, anger mixed with the pain of longing. He was tired of feeling angry. He looked at the paper again and looked at the phone but quickly lost his courage to call. Maybe if he could jump in the car, drive over to Sherman Oaks, and drive by his home; that would be enough for today. It didn't really make a lot of sense, but he suddenly felt compelled to do it.

He wrote a note and affixed it on the microwave. He had folded it with Maddy's name on the outside with the hope that Emily would not read it. He didn't want her asking why Daddy was saying he was sorry. He added that he'd be home for dinner. He got his "Thompson Brother's Guide" (a book of maps for the greater Los Angeles area) out and charted his route. The surface streets would be busy with people running errands but Frank decided to take them anyway. He wanted time to steel himself even if he was only driving by.

The apprehension rose considerably when he realized that he was on the actual block. He took no notice of how beautiful each house was or how perfectly manicured the landscaping; Jake's focus was on the ascending house numbers as well as an awareness of how fast his heart was beating. He now saw the house. Much to his own surprise he found himself parking right in front of Frank's home, if it still was his home. Jake sat in the car for a minute. He looked at the house, not noticing the lovely exterior of brick and white wood, and the swath of white flowers that spread across the front of the rambling 50s ranch. Instead, he saw his uncle's face, the smiling face that he had known as a child. And with courage he didn't know he had, got out of the car and walked resolutely up the meandering stone walk, and knocked on the paneled white door.

There wasn't an answer. Jake knocked again. His courage began to fail and he felt relieved. He turned and started walking back toward his car. He heard the door open but no voice called out. He had to look back; as much as he didn't want to, he also knew he had to. Jake turned 180 degrees and stopped. Uncle Frank stood there. His blonde hair was mixed with gray and his build was still slender. For a sixty-year-old, he looked youthful. Jake felt his uncle looking at him, drinking him in. There was a moment more of silence, and then Frank uttered, "Jake, is that you? Jake, I can't believe it's you."

"Yes, Uncle Frank; it's me."

"Good God, I knew in an instant. Just the way you were walking away, and when you turned, I knew."

Jake's reply was sincere, "You really haven't changed much, not much at all in twenty-three years."

"Come in! Come in! I'm so pleased to see you." Frank followed his uncle through the door into a foyer. "Let's just keep going through the house and out onto the patio," Frank continued. "It's a comfortable place to be this time of day." Jake noticed, as they passed the den, that there were several autographed pictures on the wall, and he was reminded of the various celebrity biographies his uncle had penned over the years.

"Sit there," suggested Frank as he pointed to a cushioned chair. "The shade's a bit cool and that will keep you in the sun." For the first time, as he glanced beyond the pool and elegant landscaping, Jake realized how exquisite the home was. For most of the past twenty-three years, when he had thought of his uncle, he seldom got beyond his anger. He had never thought about how he lived, who his friends were, anything like that. Well, not exactly true. At some point, he wondered if Frank might be gay. His memories of him didn't fit gay stereotypes, but he was a writer and it seemed like so many people in the arts were gay. And Karen had said something once, typical of her open-ended snide comments, "Someday you'll be glad that he went back to California and stayed there." The years went on, and as Jake understood how intolerant Karen was toward anyone different, he wondered.

Frank asked Jake if he wanted a beer. Jake declined. Frank disappeared into the house anyway. The air was still and dry, and Frank had been right, the heat of the sun was welcoming. Jake was still lost in his thoughts when Frank returned with two large glasses of lemonade.

"You came on the right day. I made this lemonade this morning. It's the way your grandmother used to make it, with a little sweet tea added. But I know that you didn't come here today for the special lemonade. How did this great event come about?"

Jake looked at his uncle and suddenly was overcome with the realization that he was seeing what his father would have looked like had he lived. It took him a few seconds to regroup, and then Frank smiled at him, and it took a few seconds more. Finally, he replied, "I live out here now. I'm married and have a daughter and we moved here from Chicago just after the first of the year. I was able to get your address, that's kind of a long story, and I just decided this afternoon to see if you might be home."

"Jake, this is such a wonderful surprise for me."

Jake felt delight in the compliment but then suddenly thought to himself, "Where have you been for the past twenty-three years? You always knew how to find me." Part of him really wanted to ask his uncle just that but part of him didn't want to know…at least yet.

"How's Karen?" Frank asked, as if he was reading Jake's mind. "Your mother and I have lost touch over the years."

"She's fine."

Frank remained quiet, as if he expected Jake to say more.

"Mom's very much occupied with her work."

"What is she doing? Last I knew she was an administrative assistant to some director of Thorton Industries."

"She's still at Thorton. But, if that director is still there, she may be his boss now. She's been a vice-president for the last three years."

"That doesn't surprise me. Karen has always had tremendous drive. She'd get done what needs to get done." Frank was hoping his face wasn't revealing his unspoken thoughts. Karen had tremendous drive, enough for herself and the lives of everyone around her. She was canny, too. Canny enough to disguise her turbo-ambition through the year of dating Tom before they married. Frank hadn't perceived that side of her either, and he had good instincts about that kind of thing.

"Tell her congratulations on all her success," mumbled Frank, bringing his focus back to the present. Jake didn't reply, and for the first time, there was an awkward moment between them.

Jake broke the silence. "I saw a review of your latest book in the Calendar section. Actually, my wife Maddy saw it and brought it to my attention."

"They didn't seem to like it much, but then that reviewer is always disappointed in what I find interesting in famous people's lives."

"What do you find interesting?"

"The fact that people who are viewed as larger than life have to deal with the ordinary problems that we all do. I find where they begin much more interesting than where they arrive. By the time they're famous, readers often know how their lives have unfolded. How did they get there? Why did they get there? That's infinitely more interesting. She said something about not providing readers with what they want to know. That's because I don't focus on the intimacies of my subject's relationships or expose their vulnerabilities in a simplistic kind of way.

"I'll tell you why. I have this image of a crumpled up scandal rag lying in the ditch, yesterday's trashy exposè of some famous person. Readers are no longer interested; they've moved on, looking for fresh meat. But, the subject is left wounded, and for what, a momentary thrill for total strangers to get off on. I don't want to be part of that."

There was a brief interlude and then Frank asked, "Tell me Jake, have you ever read any of my books?"

Jake's face reddened.

Frank smiled. "You don't have to answer. My guess is that you don't read celebrity biographies, period."

"No, I don't."

"I'll tell you the problem with celebrity bios. When you're finished with most of them, you have an empty feeling inside. Not just that you wasted your time but that something has been sucked out of you. There's a reason for that. No matter how hard you try, you can't make someone's bald ego attractive. Once a person becomes famous, it's easy for him or her to think that their every thought is brilliant. So many people make money from being in their orbit, often great sums of money; their acolytes cater to every whim, bow at every command.

"I remember one actress telling me, 'I used to think that all these people loved me. Years later I realized that they all hated me.' But, she had been caught up in a world where everyone was sucking up to her. The producers, the directors, even her family. At least she was smart enough to figure it out and find some degree of redemption. The point being is that no one is that interesting if their life is all about themselves."

"You don't sound like you've enjoyed your work. People would just assume that it would be great hanging out with the rich and famous."

"I did enjoy it early on. Most of these people are world-class charmers and they go all out to charm you so that you'll write a flattering book. I have to admit, that part has always been seductive."

"Who are you planning to work with on your next project?"

"Just between you and me, Jake, I don't know if there's going to be a next one."

Jake didn't know how to reply and once again an awkward silence fell. This time it was Uncle Frank who picked up the conversation. "Can you go out and have a bite to eat with me? I know every good place within a 30 minute radius."

"I wish I could but I left a note telling Maddy I'd be home for dinner. My coming over here today was a rather sudden impulse and I really need to get right back."

Frank was dying to know what had been behind that impulse, but also knew it would have to be a question asked later, if at all. He had spent his professional life knowing what questions to ask and when. "Jake, I'm so happy that you came. Promise me that you'll come back. Bring Maddy, too. And your daughter. What's her name?"

"Emily. She's seven."

Jake got up and as he shook Frank's hand, he glanced into his uncle's eyes very quickly. He wanted to see his dad in him and that's where he would see him most. Jake didn't consider how emotional the visit had been for his uncle; he could barely understand what was going on inside himself. He walked back through the house and out to his car. Looking back, Frank stood on the walk, watching him. Frank's glance sent a surge of warmth flowing through Jake's body. It triggered something but Jake didn't place it. He didn't remember that it was the same sensation he had felt when Uncle Wonderful, the name he had called him as a child, arrived from California for a visit.

Chapter 2: Sleazebag

A month later.

Jake watched the landscape guys loading their equipment. He still felt a little guilty hiring someone to mow their postage stamp size lawn. But then again, that was the point. It was so small and so cheap to have it done, it wasn't worth doing it himself. And these guys really knew more about the desert-friendly flowers and plants than he did. When Jake was growing up, Karen had expected him to take responsibility for the yard from age eight onward. Now he begrudgingly agreed to himself that she had been right about that. He grew up knowing that work was part of life. No big deal.

However, Jake was finding his position as an advertising agency account executive less than satisfying. Everyone told him how lucky he was to get that position. A friend of Maddy's uncle had set up the interview. Maddy had been ecstatic; this position would move them to her beloved Southern California. At the time, Jake thought he wanted it, too. After all, he had changed his major at DePaul to marketing in his junior year, and he now realized that there really weren't many jobs of this kind for the flood of people who wanted them.

Maddy broke into this uneasy reflection, "What time did you say you were going to your uncle's?"

"He said to come around 2:00."

Maddy was pleased. She had been surprised when she had returned home on that Saturday and Jake pulled in right behind her, saying he had been to his Uncle Frank's. Uncharacteristically, she didn't ask him much about it and characteristically, Jake didn't have much to say. Maddy sensed that something vital had taken place for Jake and she didn't want to tamper.

"Are you sure that you don't want to come along? Emily's social life won't collapse if she misses a play date."

"No, you go ahead. I have my to-do list, and you know better than to get between me and my to-do list." Jake did know better. Maddy was one of those people who got things done and that meant stay out of her way. Jake admired that quality about her. He liked order.

Truth was, Maddy's instincts told her that the right time to meet Uncle Frank wasn't now. And really, Jake felt the same way. It wasn't that Jake was particularly analytical about such matters, but something personal, something private, had been tripped on the first visit that needed further vetting.

Jake to Maddy, "I'll be back by six; are we still planning to eat out?"

"I'd prefer that if you're in agreement."

"Sure."

Jake appreciated that about Maddy. She really did care how he felt about things.

Jake arrived at Frank's at 2:00 sharp. It was another nice California day. They seemed to all be this way, one right after another. After Chicago weather all his life, Jake was getting used to this new climatic sameness. He wasn't finding it monotonous but it did seem a little unreal. And, as he looked around Frank's neighborhood, he reflected on an observation he had made about many such neighborhoods in Southern California.

Homes that had been built fifty years earlier, bungalows or ranch homes, homes for then-young families, now had a Disney quality to them. They too, were a bit unreal in that they were now maintained to perfection. Instead of streams of kids running loose, as there once must have been, it was now eerily quiet, home values inflated beyond young families' affordability. There was now a self-consciousness about these homes that reflected their owner's preoccupations with their monetary value.

Jake walked up to the door and knocked. He felt butterflies stirring in his gut but nothing like his first visit. Frank opened the door with a relaxed smile that put Jake at ease.

"I knew you'd be right on time. You probably don't remember, but your dad was that way, too." Jake absorbed the comparison but made no reply. Frank continued, "I'm also that way. And so was our dad. That's one of my memories as a kid, waiting in the car; Dad, Tom, and me, waiting for our mother who always came up with last minute things to do in the house."

Jake never knew his Grandfather Ford and had only vague memories of Grandmother Ford. Even before Tom died, Karen had done her best to discourage that tie. For that matter, Jake had seen very little of his mother's family. Jake could see now, that through Uncle Frank, he was going to learn something about his dad's family. The possibility of connecting to people, even if they were no longer alive, was appealing.

"Come in." Frank repeated the trek toward the patio and Jake followed, this time more observant of the rooms they passed through.

This was a neat house, uncomplicated. Unlike the exterior, which marched lockstep with the rest of the neighborhood in presenting its broad marketability, the interior had a quiet whisper of individuality. Some of the furniture appeared almost shabby, suggesting tales of having been around, but also spoke of comfort. There were paintings on the walls that called attention to themselves, but at the same time fit in perfectly with where they were. Jake guessed they were all originals. Some were quirkily modern, but modernity of different periods, and there were representative oils and watercolors.

"I was happy to get your phone call on Wednesday," stated Frank, well aware that in Jake's hurried departure from the first visit that phone numbers hadn't been exchanged. He knew better than to ask Jake how he had gotten the unlisted number. He was just happy to see him again. They were soon on the patio. "Sit down; that's officially your chair now. Sit down, and this time, you're going to tell me about yourself." Jake made himself comfortable and Frank continued. "You know, I've made a living listening to others, but after you left last time, I realized that, for a change, I had done most of the talking. This time it's going to be about you."

Jake felt a little uncomfortable. He really didn't like to talk about himself. People were often mistaken about Jake. With his handsome face and quick charm, people expected him to be more open. Frank, with informed sensitivity, read the situation instantly. "Jake, let me take a guess about you. People assume that you're an extrovert but you're not. You're an introvert who just happens to have pleasing social skills."

Jake found himself smiling. "Yeah, something like that."

"Well, for one thing, it's that smile. You must take a lot of people in with that," continued Frank. This made Jake's smile all the bigger. "I feel sorry for people who go through life grim-faced; they just have to work so much harder. And, speaking of work, what kind of work do you do? I didn't even ask you that the last time."

"I work as an account executive on the Marine World account. I also have responsibility for a few little accounts, but Marine World is my big focus. It's a small agency and that account is mainly what we all do."

"Killer whales, dancing dolphins, sharks swimming overhead; I've seen the commercials."

Jake laughed, "You forgot the seals balancing balls, the penguins marching like old men, the walruses looking even more like old men; just to hit the most common clichés."

"What does an account executive do?"

"In a nutshell, anything that one can do to increase attendance by 15% over the previous year."

"Do you think up the stuff? Come up with the creative ideas?"

"It's my job to sell the ideas to the client that the creative people develop. The assumption is that the client doesn't have enough good sense to recognize a good idea when he sees one. It's my job to listen to his concerns and then convince him that the agency knows best."

"I've seen your commercials. I like the one that just focuses on the sea creatures themselves accompanied by classical music."

Jake smiled again but his eyes narrowed. "That spot was the only client-driven spot that got produced. I agree that it's powerful, but I don't know how effective it is in bringing people into the gate. Did it bring you in?"

"No."

"The agency knows what they're doing. There's a formula that they follow and they just dress it differently, year after year."

"Give me an example."

"They're either peddling fun, adventure, guilt, or some combination. Here's an example. You see some little children skipping through the park, stopping to pet a dolphin here, laughing at a seal doing a double-take there, and so on. Then at the end, you see the parents looking at their happy children while the voice-over chants, 'Let them know they're special! Bring your kids to Marine World!' Unspoken message: 'What kind of parents would you be if you didn't?'"

"Not particularly subtle, is it?"

Jake's voice took on an increasingly energetic tone, obviously enjoying the conversation with someone who shared the absurd humor of advertising hyperbole. "That was the subtle one! The preferred tagline the agency had pushed was, 'Parents who love their children love Marine World.'"

"Why did they stop there?" inquired Frank mischievously. "Why not, 'Parents who love their children take them to Marine World every week.'"

"Without fail," interjected Jake, and both men laughed, shamelessly enjoying their own cleverness.

Frank interjected, "Why not, 'Parents who are saving money for the future are ignoring their children's happiness today. Particularly when today could be a day at Marine World!'"

"Uncle Frank, you've missed your calling. Maybe we could bring you in as a consultant."

"I think you could bring to the table any idea I might have to offer," retorted Frank.
"I'm glad to discover you have such a sardonic sense of humor. That will serve you well."

Jake was thinking a similar thought. It was great that Frank was as humorously disdainful as himself.

Frank continued, "Do you have someone with whom you work that laughs at the same things you do?"

"Yeah, there's a young guy on the client side who works at the Chicago Park who sees it the same way. We have a lot of laughs on the phone."

"I guess I knew that there was a Marine World in Chicago."

"That's one of the reasons I was hired. I had been knocking around the Chicago media market for a few years so they knew I knew some people. Also, they thought I could bring my 'Midwestern sensibility' to the table. I wasn't sure what they meant by that at the time, but now I think they meant someone who could keep them in check in case the message was too hip for the Midwest. I try to do my best on that front," Jake declared with a droll smile.

"Actually, I think they have a point," reflected Frank. "The Midwest is different from the West Coast and different from the East Coast as well. The West Coast is much more transient, much more defined by pop culture. I could see why they'd want someone like you weighing in. As dynamic as Chicago is, it remains a European city at heart. Family means a different thing there."

"I think I know what you mean," stated Jake. "Maddy's family is tight and they do all kinds of things together; but they seem to be an exception out here." Jake wished that he could say that he embraced Maddy's family as his own. He did like them yet he resisted being part of them. He didn't really understand why.

"Does the agency appreciate your Midwestern sensibilities?" asked Frank, bringing the conversation back to Jake's job. The question hit a nerve and Jake suddenly wanted to get something off his chest. Jake had learned growing up that it was safest to reveal as little as possible about how he felt. But there was something safe about Uncle Frank.

He blurted out, "Not really; I feel out of sync. And it's the Marketing Director from the Chicago Park with whom I'm having the most trouble. I'm doing the work. I do everything he asks. And raise hell to get it done as fast as he wants it, which is always right now. What it comes down to is that he doesn't like me and I don't like him. It's gotten to the point that my stomach turns every time I hear his voice on the phone."

"Any idea why he doesn't like you?"

"I was basically hired to be the agency gofer for him. But I think he resents that he's now supposed to talk to me instead of always having the ear of Brad, the agency president."

"Anything else?"

"Essentially, he's a sleazebag. When he comes to L.A., I'm supposed to entertain him. His idea of a good time is several martinis and dinner, then sit in the lobby of his hotel trying to spot the high-end call girls. I know after he gets rid of me, he calls an escort service. I don't care if he screws himself dizzy until the Viagra runs out. But then he looks at me with those dead eyes as if I'm some kind of loser because I'm not more a man of the world. And I know the president of the agency feels the same way. Brad told me one day that he was disappointed in me. When I asked him why, he really couldn't say other than, 'You're not really who I thought that I was hiring.' I do the work; I'm better organized than any account man in the agency so he couldn't really fault the work. As for fun, I'm an excellent golfer, but these losers don't play golf. It's frustrating!"

Frank appreciated Jake opening up to him and he had listened intently. He had learned long ago that the key to being a good listener was to really care about what the other person was saying. And he did care. After a brief silence, Frank responded, "I'm sure you don't know this, but in my checkered life, I've worked in the corporate world as well, and even though that was a long time ago I learned something valuable.

Like you, I used to feel frustrated when I did good work, everything asked of me and more, and yet I didn't feel appreciated. Then it dawned on me. I really wasn't working with adults. Not really. I began to see my boss as a scared child who was more concerned about being protected than he was about getting things done in an orderly fashion. What he really wanted from me was everything I could do that would make him look good. In a word, they want to be taken care of."

"So, doing the work and doing it well isn't enough?"

"I don't think so. It's more important to make them feel safe. The fact that you aren't interested in the hookers is conveying some sense of judgment."

Jake reacted defensively, "It's his business if he wants to be a lowlife. Why should I care?"

"The fact remains; you think of him as a lowlife and he knows that."

"So what am I supposed to do? Drink more than I want to drink? Ogle at the call girls with leering eyes? I'm not going to do that."

"I'm glad you're not.'

"Yeah, but where does that leave me? I'm still the odd man out and I don't know what to do to fix it. Working harder isn't going to change anything; you just said it."

"What do you like about these guys, your boss and the Chicago guy?"

"They're both smart. I like how quick they think."

"What else?"

"Can't think of anything else. I wish I could say that they're honest but they'd steal any idea from anyone."

"Well then, let's go back to smart. Let them know that you think they're smart. It won't be phony because you mean it. Are they good storytellers? Do you honestly laugh at their jokes?"

"My boss is totally devoid of humor. I have the impression that he doesn't allow his mind to stray more than a few seconds from the 17%

add-on-commission and the bottom line. Humor is frivolous to him. He does manage to laugh at Art's jokes. Not really laughing, more just a show of teeth. Art's the guy from Chicago."

"Is Art funny?"

"He tells stories well. He remembers intricate jokes, and hits the punch line just right."

"Enjoy him. Enjoy his jokes. Enjoy everything you can about him. He might very well see you in a different light. And, one more thing. Keep that smile going; that's a real plus for you."

Jake felt like a burden had been lifted. He didn't know if Frank's advice would be any help but it felt good just to be able to talk about it. Funny how things work out. There was something good about being with his uncle, some kind of feeling that he had known when he was little. He knew that after the first reunion, but he knew it on a deeper level now. He would be seeing a lot of his Uncle Frank.

After Jake left, Frank too knew that he'd be seeing more of Jake. That was the good news. The great news! The bad news was that he saw trouble brewing ahead for Jake.

Chapter 3: Battle with No Winners

The yellow gladiolas were beautiful. Long and elegant but without pretension, they were much like Maddy herself. Jake had driven to the downtown L.A. flower mart to find them; he knew what Maddy liked. Maddy stood looking at them, the late morning sun snuck its way through the kitchen window, creating intricate shadows on the blooms. Now looking toward the driveway, Maddy watched a shirtless Jake take a chamois across the hood of her car. He was doing the finishing touches. He was good to look at, well put together. He didn't seem to have to work at it and he didn't take his good looks very seriously.

Jake had reminded Maddy of her dad. They really didn't look alike, though they were both handsome. They both had great smiles but those weren't alike either. Her dad's was a movie star smile, with his eyes looking right into your eyes and liking what they saw. Jake had a way of dropping his head and then allowing his eyes to look up at you as if he was inviting you in. Just you. Both were seductive. But, Maddy knew her dad, and after eight years, felt she knew Jake, at least as well as you could know two men who had walls behind their smiles. Her father had been distant all through her growing up years. Maddy accepted that; that's just who he was. But, Jake… early on she had felt that she was the one person he let in and she felt almost heady at the privilege. But, Maddy hadn't felt that invitation for a long time, and a deep pang of sadness came over her. She questioned, "Who really is this man I've married?"

Jake opened the lower half of the Dutch door and strode through, flashing that smile and catching her eyes. If not the invitation Maddy had once known, it was still seductive and Maddy couldn't help smiling back. "Good," thought Jake. He had really blown it the night before. They had had it out on the way home, at least Maddy had had her say, and now it appeared that Jake was back in her good graces. He was grateful, but he always felt that maybe he didn't quite deserve her forgiveness. Maybe he didn't. The gladiolas and his washing her car weren't just peace offerings; he really was remorseful.

Jake walked over to Maddy, stopped and looked at her for a second. He wanted to drink her in. He could gloat to himself that this beautiful woman with the well-toned body, and whose clear eyes spoke of goodness, was really his wife. But right now, he felt more of an appreciation. Grateful and somewhat undeserving. He took her in his arms and kissed her, and even though he was gentle and his kiss was tender, there was an intensity that set off electric impulses that reached to Maddy's open-sandaled toes. Jake felt it too. Instinctively, they stayed in each other's arms until equilibrium returned. Then, without a word spoken, Jake held onto Maddy's arm and guided her into their bedroom.

This was another of those Saturdays that Jake had arranged to visit his Uncle Frank. As he drove across the Valley, he thought about Maddy and what a lucky guy he was. Making love with her released the most alive moments in his life and he knew it. But then thoughts of the previous evening crowded into his head. Maddy had told him a couple weeks earlier about her brother-in-law Tanner's birthday party. He had said, "Fine." But, by the time yesterday evening rolled around, he really didn't want to go. Jake suddenly felt defensive. He just wasn't in the mood to go, that's all. He liked Tanner. He liked the whole damn family; he just didn't feel like being with them last night. But he went. What more could Maddy want? So what if he was quiet? A guy has a right to be quiet. It wasn't his birthday; why was he expected to be the life of the party? He hadn't been hungry, either. Big deal. Why was all of Maddy's family so weird? They were pretending not to notice that anything was going on with him, when, really, nothing was going on with him.

Jake continued to build his defenses until the memory of Maddy's comments waved over him. Maddy was always up front. If something bothered her, you knew about it right away, or at least as soon as she found it appropriate to address the situation. They had been the first to leave and as soon as they were out of the drive, she said, "Jake, I don't understand you. This is my family. You're my husband. We're supposed to be all one family, the most important people in each other's lives." Jake had had no response and really didn't appear to be that much interested. Maddy continued, "You were so distant tonight that you were rude. If you were out to sabotage the evening for everyone, you were only partially successful. You were annoying but I think the only person that you made miserable was yourself." Jake still offered no response. "Jake, you're like a child. A pouting child. I don't really like you like this."

Jake knew better than to argue. Maddy was too clear thinking for him. He kept quiet. He wasn't able to let go of his anger, but what was he angry about? He knew Maddy was right. He was her husband. What kind of husband was he? He didn't like himself as he continued their drive home and he didn't like himself now as he was approaching Frank's house.

It was mid-afternoon. The heat of the day was uncomfortable so today they stayed inside. As Jake sat down in a rocking chair that sported a black leather cushioned seat and back, he found himself studying two portraits on the wall. Taking note, Frank asked, "Do you know who they are?"

"I can guess. The man has to be Grandfather Ford because I can see the resemblance to you and my dad. So the woman must be Grandmother Ford, even though she doesn't look like I remember her. Am I right?"

"Yes. They were both in their late thirties when they sat for those paintings. People with a little money did that kind of thing back then."

"What did he do for a living? I don't even know that much."

"Dad was a lawyer, a corporate lawyer in a small firm of which he was a principal. Dad always liked telling this story: he had a cousin who was a minister who also was more than a little crazy. One time, while Dad was still in law school, he gave Dad questionable reassurance about the hereafter. The minister told him that only 4% of lawyers go to heaven but that they were all corporate lawyers."

Jake liked the idea that his grandfather had a sense of humor. "Tell me more about him. What was he like to be around?"

"First I'll tell you that he was very smart. He grew up at a time when a lot of kids often didn't go beyond the eighth grade. Their parents needed them as workers, and, for awhile, that was as far as he got. But he was such a voracious reader and so hungry for an education that he taught himself enough to basically test out of high school. He took a few college courses as a young adult, and then went straight into law school. He was thirty when he finished."

"Was he a driven guy?"

"No, not in the way I suspect you're thinking. He was very organized and he accomplished what he set out to do. He had steel in his spine if he thought you were trying to pull a fast one, but he was quiet by nature, unobtrusive. He was really much like your dad in that way."

Jake was taking this all in. He was eager to know more about his family and a little surprised that he had known so little. He looked at the paintings again and mused, "It would have been nice to have known them. I remember seeing her when I was a kid but I just remember her being old."

"She was old when you would have remembered her. There was a missing generation there. Mom and Dad were in their thirties when they married and Mom was over forty when your dad was born. Then, your dad was twenty-eight before he got married."

"What was Grandmother Ford like?"

"She was smart, too, and loved to read. That's what they had in common. Even after we acquired our first television, I never saw her just sit and watch; she always had a book or some magazine article that was taking priority."

"So, did they have a good relationship?"

"From everything I told you so far, you'd think so. But the truth is, they didn't. When I was little it seemed like they got along okay but at some point they crossed a line and eventually they really didn't like each other."

"What happened?"

Frank reflected, "Not any one thing. I don't think one cheated on the other or anything like that. I think they were both looking for something from the other that neither was capable of giving, or they just weren't willing."

"How old were you when you realized this?"

"I don't think I was able to analyze their problems until I was a young adult. But I knew there was a problem when I was still pretty young, maybe seven or eight. I've always been sensitive about what's going on with people. That's probably how I've ended up writing the kind of books I've written."

Jake was feeling a growing discomfort with this conversation but, at the same time, felt a growing curiosity. "What kind of things were you noticing?"

"It evolved over the years. First, I think I was aware that Dad wasn't home as much. He started working later. He became more involved in civic-type organizations that took up time in the evenings. We didn't seem to do as much as a family as we had. Then I was aware that Mom started berating Dad for things that didn't make sense. He was an excellent provider, but she'd treat him like he was a loser for the way he took care of his family."

"Sounds like he was the one getting the raw deal."

"I thought that for awhile. But in time, I realized that he was a guerrilla fighter. There's a saying that the most extreme form of cruelty is indifference and he became increasingly indifferent to her. Also, Mom was always battling to take off the same twenty pounds. He said things like, 'Anne, I'm surprised to see you eating those olives,' knowing that would make her feel guilty. As he got older, he'd insist on wearing worn-out clothes to church because he knew that would get to her. It was always something between those two. I don't think I ever saw any tenderness towards each other in the last twenty-five years of their lives."

"Why did they stay married?"

"People did in those days. I remember their 40th wedding anniversary. For some reason Dad wanted to make a big deal out of it so your dad and I hosted a big dinner. I remember wondering what it was that we were celebrating. Dad died that following fall so I'm glad we did it."

Again, there was a silence. Frank could tell that this conversation was registering on some level with Jake. His intuition told him to continue on. "You know what was so sad about the whole thing, particularly since they were such intelligent people?"

Jake shook his head in a way that asked, "What?"

"They never really fought about anything that mattered. Anything that might have gotten to the bottom of their unhappiness. It was always just hurling insults, ignoring each other, a continuous wounding of each other around the edges. It became a battle, not a marriage. A battle with no winners." A sad smile edged across Frank's face. "Oh, you might say that Mom won. She lived four more years after Dad, and Tom and I used to say to each other, 'Who is this woman?' She had mellowed so much. Pretty sad, don't you think?"

Again, Jake shook his head.

Frank continued, "If only they had had the courage to pick their battles wisely, to really look deep and honestly into why they were unhappy. And it does take courage. Courage to allow yourself to be vulnerable. Courage to reach down to the pain that you don't want to feel. I think they were both too fearful to do that."

There was a silence and then Frank continued, "Jake, people have the wrong idea about vulnerability. They see it as exposing themselves to vultures. But the opposite is what happened with Mom and Dad. They wouldn't/couldn't open themselves up and instead they turned into vultures preying on each other. Instead, they traded getting to the depth of vulnerability where problems could be solved for the surface vulnerabilities where they just nipped at each other.

Jake remained quiet. He didn't like what he was hearing. It was hitting a raw nerve. He particularly didn't like the business about making yourself vulnerable. These were not ideas that he thought about on a conscious level. When it came to inner pain, he operated on instinct. Instincts got him through his lonely childhood and into his adult years. His instincts were now telling him to get away from this conversation and out of Frank's house.

Before he could think of a way to extricate himself, Frank resumed, "Jake, there was a play by Thorton Wilder titled "Our Town." My parents actually saw it on their honeymoon in New York. I won't go into the play's story, but there's a line that says something like, 'If you could really see ordinary moments for what they are, they're so beautiful, so extraordinary, that you'd barely be able to stand them.' That's what Dad and Mom missed, all those ordinary moments together. People keep thinking that they have to do something special, take the kids to Marine World, fly over to Hawaii, something out of the ordinary. In truth, it's in those small ordinary moments where life is lived to the fullest."

As soon as Jake could get away he did. He didn't want to think about picking one's battles wisely... being vulnerable... extraordinary moments... none of it. But he kept hearing Maddy say, "You're my husband. Jake, you're my husband."

What kind of husband was he? Again, he didn't want to think about any of it. But why had he been such a bastard the night before? Why was he such a bastard with Maddy so much of the time? "Goddamn," he didn't want to think about it. He heard Maddy's voice, "Jake, you're a child; I don't like you like this"... Frank saying,

"Mom and Dad got to a point where they didn't like each other."

What could he think about? Playing golf. That's what he thought about when he was a teen and working as a caddy. He thought about the good shots that he saw, and the good shots that he made when he had the opportunity to do so. But why was he so unhappy as a kid that he would try to get himself thinking about golf? All kinds of swimming thoughts were trying to enter Jake's head: thoughts about growing up and thoughts about now and they were trying to connect. Jake didn't want any part of them.

What did Frank say? Have the courage to be vulnerable? "Fuck," he didn't want to think about that either. What made Uncle Frank Mr. Fuck-you, Know-It-All? What about that shot that he had made at El Dorado Park in Long Beach last Thursday evening? That was some shot. Ninth hole, three under par. He was playing by himself but others saw it too. That was something! Really something! Jake's instincts had taken control and he was safe for now.

Frank was concerned. It was obvious that Jake was experiencing some sort of inner turmoil. He hadn't been rude. He had just stood up and said, "I have to go," and he did in a matter of seconds. Frank hadn't met Maddy yet. He wondered why.

Frank was experiencing a premonition lately that he wasn't going to live much longer. He saw this kind of feeling as self-indulgence and he didn't like self-indulgence. Nevertheless, the premonition held on. How many ordinary moments did he have left? He was hoping to share as many with Jake as he could. Too much time had been wasted.

Chapter 4: Cowboy Ty

Jake strolled across the expansive plaza of Century City and walked up the steps toward a Japanese restaurant he had passed scores of times. It was an expense account type of restaurant, and since Art, his client from Chicago, didn't like Japanese food, Jake had yet to pass through its door.

Today he was going to meet Frank for lunch, Frank's idea. There was no question that both of them would be on time. He walked in and saw Frank already seated with a welcoming smile on his face. As he approached the table, Frank spoke, "I'm glad that this could work out for you. I had to be in the area anyway and having lunch with you makes it worthwhile. I didn't think to ask you on the phone. Do you like Japanese?"

"I really like tempura," Jake replied with some exaggeration. "You can keep the sushi."

Frank grinned and then asked, "How tight is your schedule this afternoon?"

"I need to be back in the office by 1:30, not that I really have anything to do."

"Are the killer whales on strike?"

"I wouldn't care if they are. It's no longer my business," Jake uttered with an edge.

Frank queried, "What's going on?"

"I'm off the Marine World account. Art got his way and he's working directly with Brad again."

"What's that leave you with?"

""Leave me with,' is the right way to put it. I'm left with the dreg accounts. One is a hotel in Laguna Beach that doesn't have a budget worth a damn. This was Brad's first account but I'm surprised he's held on to it; I wouldn't consider loyalty as one of his stellar attributes. It's definitely more trouble than it's worth. I'm also handling Ty's Chuck Wagon restaurant chain."

Frank reflected, "Ty Moran was a big cowboy TV star. I think back in the 70s. I used to see quite a few of those around Southern California."

Jake responded in a tight-lipped manner, "I notice you're saying you 'used to see quite a few.' Now they're down to six stores and they're in locations where the real estate is cheap enough that he's able to hold on to them. And you also mentioned that his time was in the 70s. People today don't give a shit about ol' Ty Moran; most people today never heard of him. But don't tell him that."

Frank stated, "I assume you're working with him directly. What's he like?"

Jake wasn't sure how to answer. How truthful could he be? By now he had concluded that Frank was gay. He had no problem with it, but was it his place to initially tread into that territory? He decided to go for it. "Frankly, Uncle Frank, Ty Moran is a pompous old queen. His face has had so much work done that the only things moving are his eyes. He just looks silly in his cowboy boots and big silver buckle."

Frank replied, "You wouldn't know this but there was an agent in this town. Henry Wilson was his name. He was famous for his stable of young hunks, many of them reputedly gay. Ty Moran was one of them."

Jake continued, "I've walked into one of his restaurants with him and it's embarrassing. He's in his costume, and he's acting like his presence is giving everyone a thrill. No one even notices him. He can't afford TV anymore so we're pretty much reduced to print advertising, mainly coupons. But he still has to have his picture, with that big cowboy smile, on every piece. Of course he insists it be airbrushed to hell. He wants to look twenty-five, but he only looks empty."

Frank responded, "Like a sixty-year-old who hasn't learned anything from life. That's a look I've known well from my line of work, both men and women."

"And that's not the worst of it. He keeps coming onto me. Believe me; it's not my imagination. He's always touching me, his hand lingering a little too long. And when he looks at me, it's for a little too long and his stare into my eyes a little too deep. It's creepy. I keep pretending that I'm not getting it."

Frank is uncomfortable with Jake's tale of an older man hitting on a younger man. Uncomfortable because he's an older gay man, but even more because Jake's the target of the unwanted attention.

Jake continued, "The fossil cowboy doesn't know it, but Maddy's going to join us for dinner Friday night. Hopefully he'll back off when he meets her."

Frank altered the subject and said, "I'd love to meet Maddy. Let me invite you both to dinner."

Jake counters, "We should have you over; I'd like you to meet Emily, too."

"Just let me know when. I'd love to."

The two ordered and ate their lunch. Neither had a cocktail. Jake was too disciplined to have a drink in the middle of the work day, even these days when he no longer had much to do. And Frank seldom drank alcohol anymore.

They walked out into the crisp sunshine, crisp because they were close enough to the ocean with her breezes blowing the smog further inland. Frank took a look at his watch. "We still have a half hour. Want to take a walk?"

"Sure, I've always liked walking," replied Jake. Frank wondered if Jake remembered how his dad loved to walk. When Jake was little, he would ride upon his dad's shoulders for miles of Chicago sidewalks.

They headed south, down Century Boulevard, walking on the west side of the street. Frank asked, "Ever hear of a movie, *CLEOPATRA,* starring Elizabeth Taylor?"

Jake replied, "I know about the real Cleopatra. Never saw the movie." History had been Jake's first love academically. However, midway through college he was advised to switch to marketing as a better career move.

"The reason I'm mentioning CLEOPATRA has something to do with the street we're on. The movie had huge production problems and went way over budget. It put 20th Century-Fox into such dire financial straits that they had to sell off their back lot. What you see all around was once that back lot."

"Including Century Boulevard?"

Frank shook his head affirmatively. "Also the office tower you work in, these office buildings right here, and the condo complex across the street. In this building to the right is where President Reagan had his offices after he came back from Washington." Jake looked at the postmodern brown granite building, apparently taking an interest.

Frank continued, "Of course, much of the history on this ground has to do with the movie industry. I'm still fascinated by it, particularly the era considered the Golden Age of Hollywood. Are you much into movies, Jake?"

"Some of them. I like sports so I like movies about sports."

"Did you go to the movies much as a kid?"

"Not a whole lot. Sometimes my friend Jonathon and I would go."

"Jake, I can see we're on different wave-lengths. When I was a kid, it was the movies that seemed real, not the life that was going on around me. The movies and television both. I told you how Dad and Mom used to fight all the time and how sensitive I was to what was going on between them. I used to watch *Father Knows Best* on TV. It aired Wednesday nights and Jim and Margaret Anderson never fought about anything. They were just focused on solving the problems their kids seemed to get into week after week. Then on Sunday afternoon, I almost always went to our neighborhood theater for the matinee. I knew who all these actors were. I knew all about them, or at least the larger than life images that the studio had created for them."

"Did my dad go to these movies with you?"

"Not very often. He was like you, more into sports. And Tom had more friends. I think that was because he was so good in sports." Frank paused as if his mind took him somewhere else, then he continued, "Whatever reason, he had a lot more friends."

Jake realized that he hadn't been like his dad, at least as far as having lots of friends. He felt a sudden loneliness.

Frank continued, "I know lots of things about the Golden Era stars who I met in their later years, significant things that happened while they were working on this back lot. There was an actress named Loretta Young and she was making a film with Clark Gable. Have you ever heard of Clark Gable?"

"I think so."

Frank gave a passing thought to how fleeting fame can be and continued. "Loretta Young and Clark Gable were making *CALL OF THE WILD*. The crew had been in Washington State filming because it was supposed to be Alaska, and they needed lots of snow. The problem was there was too much snow; it never stopped snowing. So they came back to 20th Century's back lot and recreated Alaska.

"There was one scene that took place in a studio-constructed stream. The day they were filming that scene was the day that Loretta Young told Clark Gable that she was pregnant with his baby. Actually, he told her. Someone had asked her before getting into the water, if she was having her period. She replied, "No," that it was late. Gable overheard this and, as soon as he could talk to her privately, asked her if she thought that she might be pregnant. In those days, that would have created a big scandal since he was married. There was a moral's clause in all the stars' contracts that said if they were involved in scandal, their contracts would be revoked. Well, it turned out she was pregnant. In a series of clever maneuvers managed by her mother, she had the baby in secret. Then, some months later, gave the appearance of adopting a child as a single mother. But in reality, it was her own child."

"When did all this happen?"

"That was back in the mid-thirties. Hollywood's done a 180 on scandal since then." Jake wasn't so interested in tales of old movie stars but was gentleman enough to listen.

Frank went on, "There was another actress named Alice Faye; she was 20th Century-Fox's big musical star in the 30s. I attended a dinner party where she and Loretta, who by this time were both in their 80s, also attended. As Loretta arrived, I remember hearing Alice, in her husky voice, uttering, "Goodie, goodie, here comes Loretta Young." I don't know what that was about, but I do know Loretta had occupied the #1 dressing room at the studio. Can you imagine, professional jealousies still smarting 60 years later?"

"So, you knew a lot of these people?"

"Quite a few. I knew them long after their glory years. But, you know something, Jake? These were the actors I wanted to know. They represented the Hollywood I had thought was so real. Of course, it wasn't. But, in those days, they created heroes. There was right and wrong. I think, more than anything, there was order; a safe place for a sad child to go on a Sunday afternoon. It was clear cut, not the guerilla warfare I knew at home."

Jake looked ahead. Pico Avenue intersected at the south end of Century Boulevard and just beyond lay a golf course. And as Frank continued talking about old movie studio lore, interspersed with his troubled childhood, Jake thought back about the game he had played on that course. It was shortly after he had moved to California and started working at the agency. "Hell," he didn't want to start thinking about the agency. "Now just how did that game go?" he asked himself. He remembered whom he had been playing with, and he remembered the scores, and everything started falling into place. Jake was now feeling safe.

As they approached the end of Century Boulevard, Jake sensed that maybe Frank had stopped talking a while ago. Frank punctured the silence. "Let's just walk around the corner and look into the studio gate."

When they did, Frank explained, "What you're looking at is the street they built for *HELLO DOLLY*. It's supposed to be the turn of 20th century Yonkers." Jake felt naked. He couldn't give a damn and knew that it showed. They retraced their steps to Century Boulevard and headed back toward Jake's office.

Jake couldn't shake the naked feeling. And, worse, he could see the twin Century City towers sticking up above all the buildings in front of them. His mind turned to the office he now dreaded more than ever. He hated walking through those double doors with the agency's name spread across in just the right color, size, and font. They walked in silence for several minutes. Jake wished now that Frank would start babbling about old movie star stuff, about anything.

In a few minutes, they were at the fountains in the middle of the boulevard. Jake said, "I guess I better get back. I'll check the copy, then send off the latest print ads to Ty so that he can inspect for any minuscule lines around his mouth."

The two said goodbye, and Jake walked toward his office. Frank looked at his watch: 1:20 P.M. His appointment was in the building just ahead of him. He had 10 minutes to get there; he'd make it on time.

Frank reflected back on his words about how the movies of his youth had made him feel safe, at least for a couple of hours on a Sunday afternoon. He knew that contemporary filmmakers viewed that era and its movies as inherently dishonest. Maybe they were. There were lots of social issues shoved under the carpet not to be examined, homosexuality being one. But, at the same time, Frank wondered if in their quest for honesty, current filmmakers created main characters that were too self-absorbed. "How was that helping anyone?" he mused. As for himself, he missed the varnished heroes of his youth.

Then a wry grin spread on his face. It dawned on him that his focus on movies was still serving him as a distraction. He hadn't wanted to think about this appointment. He was used to facing facts but he was in avoidance about this. He had been calling it a premonition, one that he wasn't going to indulge. But, had he really been feeling more fatigued? He had always been in good shape but he was now feeling beat up after the short walk to Pico Avenue and back. He was losing weight, too. Finally, he had called his doctor, an internist, and set the appointment.

Frank knew himself well. Telling old movie star tales to someone who wasn't interested wasn't him. He didn't like not being himself. It was time to get to the bottom of things.

Chapter 5: Second Strike

Frank enjoyed the subtle sounds of quiet. He liked hearing the hum of the refrigerator and the drone of the fan of the cooling system; he particularly liked the sound of the dryer with its irregular tumbling rhythm. When he was a boy, he had liked standing still in the backyard, enraptured by the sudden sound of birds and the movement of the trees that eluded him when he was in full motion and his mind was elsewhere. Today, however, as he lay on the sofa in his den, he was all nerves. He was apprehensive that the next sound he would hear would be the ring of his phone, announcing a call from his doctor that he did not want to receive.

His doctor's name was Michael. He and Frank had been close friends for a number of years and one evening while they were at dinner, Michael said, "Frank, would you like it if I became your primary care doctor?"

Frank replied, "Of course, I would. I just never wanted to put you in the awkward position of having a professional relationship with someone that you are close to personally. But, yes, that would be great as far as I'm concerned."

Michael responded, "No doctor really likes to admit this, but to be honest with you, I think I'd take better care of you because I do care about you personally. Also, you wouldn't have to make an appointment for everything. You can just call me at home if all you need is a prescription called in. I'll be glad to do that." Frank was grateful for the invitation.

He had gone to see Michael the day he had lunch with Jake. Michael made arrangements for Frank to have a series of blood tests. As they drew tube after tube, it seemed as if they used every color of tube plug available, with each color designating different tests. Michael had asked him if he wanted to make an appointment to get the results and Frank had responded, "No, just give me a call, that would be fine." Michael thought he'd have results back by Tuesday afternoon. He'd give him a call one way or the other.

Since that day, Frank was much more conscious of his fatigue. It was as if the blood draw had also drained his denial that something was wrong. He now knew there was. But what?

The phone rang, and a surge of panic shot through Frank. He reached over and picked up the phone. "Hello."

"Uncle Frank?"

"Yes, Jake, how are you?"

Jake replied with his own question, "Are you okay? You don't sound like yourself."

"Yes, Jake, I'm fine." Frank was expecting the invitation to dinner that Jake had mentioned at lunch, but that's not what followed.

"Uncle Frank, they fired me yesterday; they threw my ass out. And it was Ty's fault."

"Can you come over and talk about it?"

"Yeah, maybe that would be a good idea. I've already contacted a radio station that needs an experienced sales person. I have an appointment with them at 2:00. Would it be okay if I dropped by after that?"

"Jake, if you don't know it by now, get it in your head. You are always welcome here, any time day or night."

"Thanks, Uncle Frank. I'll see you later."

"Jake, one more thing. It's always good before an interview to go through some deep breathing exercises, and take a little walk if you have time."

"Yeah, I have some time. Thanks."

Frank had heard the anxiety in Jake's voice and he hoped he could calm himself so that he presented himself well for his interview. Frank reflected, "The funny thing about interviews, they want you to be all confidence, but at the same time, hungry and a bit wired." Jake would certainly have the "a bit wired" part down.

Frank continued thinking about Jake. He hated seeing this person, whom he had loved as a child and was now growing to love as a young man, having to go through so much turmoil. But he also knew that the struggles of life make people strong, not their successes. He knew that, but it didn't make it any easier to witness. His mind continued on Jake when the phone rang once again. He had forgotten about expecting a call from Michael, and this being the case, he answered the phone casually.

"Frank, this is Michael."

Although the panic surge returned immediately, Frank was an expert at creating the manifestation of calmness. "Yes, Michael. Find out anything?"

"To be honest, Frank, I'm not sure. It could be a couple of different things. We need to get you back for some more tests."

"What do you think is going on?"

"No question that there are irregularities in the blood. Your blast cells aren't getting a chance to mature."

"Michael, you know I don't have a clue what blast cells are. What is it you don't want to tell me?"

"Your blast cells are the early stage of your blood cells in your bone marrow before they reach full maturity. Frank, if I started guessing now, I really wouldn't be a responsible doctor or friend. Can you come in tomorrow for more tests?"

"Sure, Michael. And, I know that you're a great doctor and a great friend so I respect your need for reservation at this point. But you can imagine where this is leaving me."

"Yeah, I know, or I think I do. I'll tell you what; I'll set the tests up in the morning. Be at the hospital by 8:00. Then I'll lean hard on them all day, and we can get together tomorrow night and discuss it."

"Thanks, Michael. I appreciate it." As they hung up, Frank knew that Michael felt that the diagnosis would be ominous. Michael didn't ask him to get together tomorrow night; he had told him that they would. Frank remembered his advice to Jake about taking deep breaths to calm himself down. He now realized that it would be a good idea to do the same.

His attempt at relaxation didn't work and Frank soon found himself in a freefall of emotion. Suddenly, he ached for Eddie, his former lover that had been in his life for ten years. That had ended seven years earlier and he had only seen him once since then. But now, knowing that something was wrong with him, that he might very well be dying, he missed the intimacy he had known with Eddie.

This was quickly becoming one of the most miserable days of his life. And in a little while, Jake would be arriving, full of more bad news. Frank thought about it. It wouldn't do any good to mention anything to Jake about his precarious health situation. For one thing, he didn't really know what was going on. For another, Jake was in his own freefall. Poor kid, he hadn't had an easy time of it.

Then a fresh realization crossed Frank's mind. "I don't have to be sitting here getting myself worked into a state of nerves. I have someone coming over who needs me." Frank was surprised at how having that awareness took some of the fear away. "Eddie was a long time ago, let that go." And, since Jake first walked up his sidewalk, hadn't he been telling himself how grateful he was? "Well, he's going to be walking up this sidewalk again in a few hours." In the meantime, he would take a few laps in the pool, something that would relax him far better than taking deep breaths.

When the doorbell rang, Frank greeted Jake as if he hadn't a care in the world. Jake, on the other hand, looked like he hadn't slept for twenty-four hours, which was probably the case. Nevertheless, he looked impeccable in his navy colored suit, white shirt, and red tie, somewhat formal by Southern California standards, but appropriate for a job interview.

"Like the red tie," observed Uncle Frank with a smile.

"Yeah, I've read that it's good for interviews. Something about being assertive and getting things done."

"Well, you get things done; the tie doesn't lie."

"Yeah, I get things done and they still throw my ass out."

"Have you had any lunch today?"

"No, I didn't feel like eating before the interview."

"Well, how did the interview go?"

"I think I'll probably get it. They were gaga over my experience of selling time for WGN in Chicago."

"That was a powerhouse station even when I was growing up. So, whom are you talking to here in L.A? I forgot to ask you on the phone."

"KLF."

"I know who they are, 'All talk. All the time.'"

"Yeah," Jake noted with minimal enthusiasm.

Frank interjected, "Let's get you something to eat. Come into the kitchen and we'll throw a sandwich together."

The two men strolled through the swinging door and Jake made himself comfortable. Frank resumed, "My selection is somewhat limited and you'll just have to take what you can get." Frank threw some bacon into a skillet and then searched in the refrigerator for lettuce and tomato. "Jake, what would you rather talk about, the old job or getting this new one?"

"I need to tell you about Ty. Remember last week when I told you that he's been coming on to me? I was going to bring Maddy to dinner with us Friday night to set him straight." Jake chuckles, "Boy, was that ever a poor choice of words."

Frank just listened and Jake continued, "It freaked him out. I don't know what he had in mind… actually I do, but it's too disgusting to think about. Anyway, when I walked in with Maddy, he acted real injured toward me, like something had been going on and now I was dumping him. He treated Maddy like she was a cheap trick cutting in on his action. It was bizarre and very uncomfortable for all of us. It was a short evening.

"Dumb fuck that I am, I didn't see what was coming Monday morning. Ty had called Brad at home on Sunday and told him that he just couldn't work with me, that I was rude to him and treated him like shit. Either get rid of me or the account walks. Not that the account is worth a damn anyway. But Brad said that this was my second strike with a client, and in the agency game, you don't get a third. Just like him to use some trite baseball analogy. There's a reason why he isn't on the creative side of the agency."

"What does Maddy think about all of this?"

"She was astounded by what happened Friday night. It's not that she's naïve; she grew up out here and knows what goes on. She found Ty really 'pathetic;' that was her word, and she felt sorry for him. That was until I was fired yesterday. Now she refers to Ty as a predator. At first Maddy wanted me to file a sexual harassment suit against the agency, and Ty as well. Now we both agree that we want to walk away from all of it as fast as we can."

"I agree with you there. You probably don't have a case against the agency, and it would be hard to prove anything against Ty. It would be your word against his. Plus, what you told me about the state of the restaurants; it sounds like his fortune has dwindled."

Frank completed assembling Jake's sandwich and asked, "Want a beer?"

"Yeah, I do. I'll probably have a few before the night's over."

"There's been many beers drunk, sitting on that chair and leaning on that table."

"Uncle Frank, I can see that there's a lot I don't know about you."

"There is a lot you don't know about me, that's true," replied Frank. "But I'm not the beer guzzler I was referring to. That table belonged to my Irish grandparents, my mom's parents. They bought those oak chairs secondhand at the turn of the last century. He was running a tavern at the time they got married. One big problem: he was an alcoholic. But, that's another story. I want to know how you're feeling about losing the agency position and getting this new one."

Jake thought to himself, "Here we go about feelings again." But then he realized the reason he had come to Uncle Frank's was to get some things off his chest. He responded, "To be honest, I feel like a damn loser. I've never been fired from anything and this feels like crap."

"You feel violated emotionally and physically. You feel lightheaded, like you've been socked a good one, and now you're trying to regain your balance."

"Yeah, how do you know?"

"I've been fired before. I think during one of our early visits I referred to my checkered past and that's certainly true regarding my career. When I was in college, I decided that I wanted to write plays. To put it another way, I didn't feel I was good at writing anything other than dialogue, and plays seemed the natural thing for me. Plus, I really liked plays. I liked the power that a few words could imprint. I remember watching Chekhov's "The Cherry Orchard" as a young man. There was a line that the mother spoke that started out frivolously but ended in great pathos, and I marveled that one sentence could do that much.

"I wanted to be the next Chekhov or Eugene O'Neil so I headed to New York to join the legion of the greats. In the meantime, I had to make a living. I delivered furniture for Macys, was a waiter near Wall Street, was a doorman on the Upper West Side, and this was before it became prestigious to live there. Eventually, I worked as a night auditor for a financial house, all the time writing my plays which have yet to be produced. My criteria was always to have time during the day to write and push my plays."

"Why so many jobs?"

"I got fired from Macy's for dropping a table and scratching the legs. The waiter job put me in touch with the guy who hired me as a doorman. I lost the doorman job because someone's brother-in-law wanted it. While I was looking for something new to do, a guy in the building where I had been doorman tracked me down and asked if I'd help him with his biography. Being rich wasn't enough; he wanted fame. His life was colorful enough and he had contacts in the publishing world so the book got published. Before I knew it, I had a new career, which eventually brought me out here and into the movie world that had fascinated me as a kid. But you know all about that."

"But then, you were on your way."

"Yes, but the road hasn't been smooth. Several times I've been under consideration as a collaborator. Then I'd meet with the subject of the proposed autobiography, and he or she decided that the chemistry wasn't right. And there were books written that were total flops. Lots of hills and valleys in my working life and that brings me to a point that I want to make. Looking back, some of my biggest failures have turned out to be my biggest successes. That's because I learned that failure doesn't have to mean that you stay down. I've always been able to get up and start something new. That's gone on my whole working life. Starting again isn't a scary thing to do when you've done it a number of times."

"I guess that's what I'm doing right now, starting again. It's not fun."

"You'll do just fine."

The conversation drifted to other subjects. Jake had a second beer and left, and Frank was alone once again. His thoughts drifted to his blood disorder of unknown origin. "You can always start over again," he had told Jake. Was he facing a predicament where that was no longer true?

Chapter 6: Michael

It was 8:00 A.M. the following morning and Frank was sitting at the hospital station where Michael had told him to report. As he was waiting for a nurse to surface, a distant figure, walking down the long corridor, caught his attention. It was Michael. Michael was short, and maybe because he was, he kept himself wiry and lean. He had been the Air Force handball champion in Southeast Asia when he was a young officer. Now in his fifties, he continued to play at least twice a week. Michael had thick hair, still mostly dark, that he had cut every two weeks because he knew that his hair was one of his best features. His eyes were dark as well and Frank felt their gaze as Michael approached. Maybe that's why he had looked up, in the same way you look over at the next car when you're waiting for a light, somehow feeling eyes upon you.

"Good Morning, Frank," Michael intoned. "I wanted to see you before I head into the office."

"That's really thoughtful of you Michael," Frank replied with a quiet smile, knowing that there was more to Michael's being there.

"Actually Frank, I've decided that I want to admit you as an in-patient. There are a couple more tests I want to run and one of them requires in-patient follow-through. I want to do a PET scan and that requires injecting a radioactive tracer into your body."

"What are you looking for, Michael?" Frank asked with characteristic calmness.

Michael didn't have Frank's demeanor. His Mediterranean heritage brought his feelings much closer to the surface and the sudden combination of sadness and fear that crossed his face prepared Frank for what came next. "We're looking to rule out some forms of cancer, Frank."

Frank felt a wave of shock but he wasn't surprised. His mom had died from cancer and Tom, too. He died from lung cancer even though he had never smoked. "What kind of cancer are you thinking, Michael?"

"As I said, Frank, at this stage we're still trying to rule things out, but you had mentioned some pain in the groin and some swelling of the nodes of your neck; so we're hoping we can rule out Hodgkin's disease or Non-Hodgkin's lymphoma."

Frank's ability to read people's faces saw right through Michael. He said, "But, you really don't expect them both to be ruled out, do you?"

The sadness which had never left Michael's eyes now only deepened. "No."

Frank looked at his distressed friend and said, "You're a great friend, Michael, my best friend. I am so lucky to have you in my life." Michael reached over and squeezed Frank's hand. The gesture, meant to communicate affection, instead relayed apprehension, a catalyst that released Frank's own gushing anxiety. It was a horrible, overwhelming feeling.

After reading the blood tests the day before, Michael knew he wanted Frank to check in as an in-patient, but had decided not to tell him until the following morning. Why put them both through a sleepless night? His concern was more than that of a doctor caring about a friend. Michael loved Frank. More than that, he was in love with Frank and had been for five years. Early on, Frank had made it clear that his feelings weren't reciprocal; he was too honest to be ambiguous on that score.

Michael had had his share of relationships. Sometimes he had left, other times he was left, but mostly he had done the leaving. He never had trouble moving on. Before Frank, the idea that he could be a casualty of unrequited love would have been laughable. During the past five years he continued to date but hadn't been able to shake himself loose. In the last year, he had given up trying. What was it about Frank that attracted him so? You could round up the usual suspects: kindness, honesty, humor… the attributes that usually come after the physical pull has diminished. They were all there. Add to that *fun*. It was important to Frank to have fun and he made a point to do so, regardless of what else was going on in his life. Maybe it was because he had never known anyone so comfortable in his own skin. What he was clear about was this: when he fell asleep at night, Frank was the man he wanted to hold or be held by. He had ached for that, five years running.

Before the day was over, Frank had undergone a CAT scan as well as the PET scan. He was then sent to a private room where the staff treated him as if he were a space alien, wearing special aprons and handling his urine as if it could set off a nuclear explosion. The tests exhausted him, though when asked if he wanted a sleep aid, he said yes.

The next morning, Michael entered the room with a grave face. "Frank, the tests both point in the same direction: Non-Hodgkin's lymphoma. Dr. Ann Steiner is going to be here in a few minutes. She's the best person I know in this field, and she has agreed to take you as a patient."

Frank was calm. "What can you tell me about it?"

"Dr. Steiner will give you the official explanation, but in essence, your body is producing abnormal lymphocytes and they're not cycling out like normal lymphocytes. Instead, they're continuing to grow and divide and then crowding into your lymph nodes. That's why you've been feeling the pain in your groin and your neck."

"Am I going to survive this thing, Michael?"

"The odds that you will are getting better every day."

Frank immediately caught the finessing of that statement, but he didn't press for clarity. Instead, he simply asked, "So, what's the treatment?"

"We're going to have to let Dr. Steiner make those decisions."

A few minutes later, Dr. Steiner entered the room. After sufficient niceties and more elaboration of the diagnosis, she discussed treatment. "Our initial treatment will be radiation with the goal of killing the cancer cells. If we're early enough, that should wipe out the majority of the cancer. Then we'll clean up with chemotherapy, injecting a combination of drugs. Mr. Ford, all this must be administered to you as an in-patient." Dr. Steiner smiled confidently and asked if there were any other questions.

"How long will the radiation treatments last?"

"We'll do one a day for 12 days."

"Any time off for good behavior?"

Dr. Steiner laughed, "If you're very, very good, we'll let you go home after the radiation for a few days to rest up for the first round of chemotherapy."

"When do we start?"

"This afternoon. I've already checked the schedule and they can get you in at 3:00. Is that alright with you?"

"Let's get the show on the road."

Dr. Steiner's confident smile never left her face for long. Frank theorized that maybe one of the reasons she was considered top in her field was that she gave her patients hope. She had made him feel more hopeful. What a cascade of emotions that passed over him in twenty-four hours! He had gone from knowing nothing, getting shot up with radioactive substances, obtaining a diagnosis, and now starting treatment this afternoon. He was dizzy from the enormity of it all.

Michael was still in the room. "Are you okay, Buddy?"

Frank replied, "I'm okay." But then looking away from Michael he added, "I have cancer. I mean, I have cancer. I just have to hear myself say it."

Frank endured the twelve days of radiation like a trooper. They exhausted him more than he had ever felt in his life, but he managed to be in good spirits when Michael stopped by every evening to visit. Michael had managed to get Frank's car back to his home and was there on the twelfth day to take him home.

Michael had a vintage black 1955 Porsche. Frank liked to think of it as the same kind of Porsche that James Dean had driven. It was the right year but wrong model. Dean had a Silver Porsche Spyder and this was a 356A Speedster. Michael couldn't have cared less about James Dean, but he was crazy about his car. He and Frank used to take long Sunday afternoon drives around Southern California. Sometimes they'd drive to Palm Springs and Frank loved when they took a long cut on the Ortega Highway through the mountains. Michael loved it too; he loved the sound of the changing gears. That was power he was hearing, and it was all at his fingertips.

Michael also had a contemporary Porsche 911 that he drove during the week, but today he had the Speedster because he knew that Frank would prefer it. It was a beautiful afternoon and Michael asked Frank if he'd like a drive through Topanga Canyon, another one of Frank's favorites. But Frank had begged off, saying he was a little tired. Michael understood but he found himself wondering if they'd ever drive through Topanga Canyon again.

Jake hadn't been in touch with his uncle since he started work at KLF. They had called the day after the interview and asked him to start right away. The first week he had been busy getting himself organized. He studied the format and the demographics it attracted, all the while turning on the charm toward the people he would be working with. The second week he started knocking on agency doors, as well as clients large enough to have their own in-house agency. Then there were those clients whose budgets were so small that no agency would waste time with them.

He wasn't picking up good vibes. The morning drive talent for KLF, their big draw, was a duo talk team that had been entertaining Los

Angeles since the late 80s. That was the problem. They were tired, and more so, their listeners were tired. What the advertisers wanted were younger listeners who were more likely to spend their money freely. Ben and Jay's listeners tended to be north of forty, just a few years shy of denture adhesive and motorized scooters that would make shopping a joy. Media markets are all about trends and KLF was trending flat. The marketing director was looking at this hotshot guy from WGN in Chicago to bring in new revenue. Jake was feeling the pressure.

Jake felt twisted up inside and he took these frustrations home. Whatever Maddy wanted from him, he wasn't willing to give, even if it was just a simple smile when she walked into a room. Jake could see what he was doing but he felt helpless, and the contempt he felt for himself did nothing to make things better.

Now Maddy was insisting that they go to couple's counseling, and that was the last thing he was willing to do. Why did everyone insist that he talk about his fucking feelings? He sensed his world closing in on him. Maybe it was time to go visit Uncle Frank.

When Jake called and asked if he could drop by, Frank made up his mind that he would tell Jake about his diagnosis. Jake lost his dad without knowing what was coming and Frank wanted Jake to be prepared for what might be happening to him. He wasn't looking forward to that conversation. Frank long ago realized something about himself. He made a living asking questions of others, often very personal questions, and he was perfectly comfortable doing so. Talking about himself was a different matter. Maybe that was why he was such a good listener.

He heard Jake's car stop at the curb and went to the door to open it. When he saw the tortured look on Jake's face, he knew that the revelation regarding his diagnosis would have to wait for another day. As Jake approached, Frank was his old self. "Welcome, my boy. I so appreciate these visits."

"Hi, Uncle Frank."

"Can I get you a beer?"

"Oh, yeah!" he said emphatically.

Jake was following his uncle when Frank stopped suddenly and asked, "Jake, do you remember what you called me as a kid?" Jake shook his head negatively, but apparently wasn't curious enough to pursue the subject.

He followed Frank into the den where he had noted the celebrity-autographed photos on his first visit. They had never sat in here before. Jake also noticed two bookshelves in the service of a couple hundred DVDs, none of the titles being familiar. "They must be all old stuff," he thought to himself.

Frank returned with a beer for Jake and lemonade for himself. "This is where I live. I've noticed that people who live in large homes, say in Beverly Hills, Brentwood or Bel Aire, tend to find a small space where they actually spend their time. I'm the same, only on a smaller scale."

"We don't have that problem in our house. The living room is it and it's small."

"See, you have what the celebs have without realizing it." Frank could see that this banter was just making Jake more anxious so he asked, "What's going on, Jake?"

"My new job sucks."

"What sucks about it?"

"For starters, Ben and Jay. You know who they are, don't you?"

Frank replied, "'Ben and Jay, the dudes who put whack into wacky' or something like that. I remember that billboard from years ago."

"Years ago, that's the problem. Everything about these guys is retro including themselves. I'm embarrassed to be out trying to sell them."

Frank said, "They must still have some faithful listeners. You're selling time. What difference does it make who fills it?"

Jake remarked, "You know what I've learned the last two weeks? If I'm going to stay in this business out here, I really need to learn Spanish and sell for Spanish-speaking stations. You realize that the top 3 stations in the Los Angeles market are Spanish-speaking? What the hell am I doing here?"

"Jake, you're going to have to answer that question for yourself."

"I don't know what the fuck I'm doing here. That's the problem."

"What about Maddy? This is her home. Isn't that why you're here?"

"It may be for her, but she dragged my ass out here and nothing's gone right for me since. It was her uncle's friend that got me the loser job at the agency, a job that I hated every day."

"Jake, are you letting Maddy help you?"

Jake shot back defensively, "What do you mean by that?"

"Jake, I'll tell you what I mean. Are you letting her help you or are you taking it out on her?"

"Fuck, damn, you know everything, don't you! Of course, I'm taking it out on her. Are you satisfied?"

"I just want you to get your priorities straight. Your job can go to hell; don't lose a marriage over it. You can find a better job; you can move back to Chicago, but don't let a good marriage go."

"How do you know that it's such a good marriage? You've never ever met her!"

"Because you told me."

After a difficult silence, Jake responded, "I know that you're right, but I don't know what to do. Maddy's insisting on couple's counseling; I just can't do that now."

"Now's the best time, Jake. It's when you're feeling the most raw that you have the most to work with."

"Fuck all that. I'm tired of feeling like shit, okay? End of story."

"That's not the end of the story, Jake. For your sake, I wish it were. You'll hate it but it will do you a world of good."

"Well, I'm not going to do it!"

"Why, Jake? What are you afraid of?"

"Don't you goddamn understand, it would kill me!"

Both men were silent at this admission. Jake didn't understand why he said it; he didn't want to know, but it scared him. Frank looked at his nephew and saw the six-year-old boy that he left behind at a Chicago cemetery. If Jake didn't understand it, Frank thought that he did; he had a glimpse of it all along but it was half hidden by shadows. He knew what Jake needed to do.

"Jake, if you really want to find out what's going wrong in your marriage, you're going to have to take a trip to Chicago."

"Now what the hell are you talking about?" Jake was feeling like a cornered-rabbit with predators coming at him from all directions.

"I could tell you but it will do you the most good if you go back and figure it out for yourself."

"Now, we have fucking riddles! I don't need a fucking riddle!"

Frank simply repeated, "Go back to Chicago and find out."

Jake shot up on his feet, "Fuck you. Who made you Mr. Goddamn-Know-Everything-About-Everybody? What do you know?" He walked out of the den and Frank followed him. "You've always had an answer for everything. Answer me this: What are you afraid of? You're always by yourself in this museum of a house, hiding out here, watching your old movies about a world that never existed. You need to get out more; you look like shit." With that, Jake slammed the front door and left.

Chapter 7: Jake the Lover

Within the hour, Michael stopped by, just as he
had visited every evening in the hospital. His
final round now took him to Sherman Oaks, the
opposite direction from his condo in Marina Del
Ray. Frank didn't discourage him, he found
himself nourished by his friend's concern. After
the firestorm with Jake, this evening's visit
would be particularly welcome. Frank had
wanted his last night at home before starting the
chemotherapy, to be relaxing and it had hardly
started out that way.

Michael had only been in the door for a minute
when he commanded, albeit with a smile, "Grab
a sweater; it's cool this evening. I'm going to
take you to dinner." What he wasn't saying was,
"You're not going to feel like eating for the next
couple of weeks. Let's not miss this opportunity
tonight."

Frank responded, "You know, I think that's a
good idea. I do feel a need to get out of this
place." Jake's words about his wandering

around his museum had strangely stung him. "Where are we going?"

"Anywhere you want. We could go down to Orange County or up to Ventura, or any place in between. Only, if we're going to be taking a long drive, I'll put the top down so you better grab a jacket instead of a sweater." Michael would do anything for Frank. Anything.

"Michael, do you remember that little Italian place in Belmont Shore? I wonder if it's still there."

"It is. I was in Belmont Shore a couple of months ago. "I walked right by it."

"Would that be okay?"

"Go get your jacket." Before Frank returned, the doorbell rang. "Do you want me to get it?" he asked in a louder voice.

"Yeah, please," shouted Frank. I can't find what I'm looking for," which was unusual because his closets were as organized as the rest of his house.

Michael went to the door and opened it to find a startled Jake on the other side. Just by looking at him, Michael knew who he was. Frank had discussed Jake often since they had reconnected. "Hi, I'm Michael Martone. You must be Jake."

"Yeah."

"I'm a friend of your uncle's. He'll be out in a minute."

Jake felt doubly uneasy. He had come back to apologize and now there was this stranger complicating things. "I only plan to stay a minute. There's just something I want to tell him."

Michael could sense Jake's discomfort. "Well, your timing's perfect. Frank and I were going to go out to eat. Would you like to join us?" Michael was hoping that Jake wouldn't.

"No, I can't. I really can only stay a minute."

Frank came down the hall from the bedrooms and saw the two men. "Jake, I see you've met my good friend, Michael."

"Yeah. Uncle Frank," Jake hesitated. It was hard for him to apologize in front of someone else, but he proceeded anyway. "Uncle Frank, I know you're on your way to dinner, but I just wanted to say I'm sorry for what I said a little while ago. All you were trying to do was help. I know that."

"Jake, apology accepted. We don't need to revisit anything,"

Frank's reply was accompanied with a sincere smile, and relief flowed over Jake's face as he turned toward the door. He said, "I'll call you in a couple of days."

"Hold up a second, Jake. I won't be here in a few days. To quote a keen observer, I do 'look like shit,' and there's a reason. I was diagnosed a few weeks ago with Non-Hodgkin's lymphoma. I'm going to start chemotherapy in the morning."

Jake's face turned white. "What does that mean?"

For once, Frank's command of saying the right thing at the right time failed him. "We'll just have to wait and see, Jake," he uttered feebly.

"Jake, I'm a doctor as well as Frank's friend." Michael reached into his jacket pocket. "Here's my card. I can keep you abreast of how the treatment is going."

Frank was relieved at this intercession. "That's a good idea; thanks Michael."

Without knowing what he was doing, Jake walked across the room and put his arms around his uncle and placed his head on his shoulder. From somewhere deep, he felt an impulse to cry. But he never cried; he couldn't remember the last time he cried, and that impulse was immediately checked. Then he wanted to say something but couldn't think clearly enough to find the words. Instead, he pulled himself away.

Frank simply said, "Thanks, Jake."

Jake once again walked toward the door, but before reaching for the knob, pulled a card out of his pocket and gave it to Michael. Everything about Jake was tight, his movements, his face, even his voice had a little too much control. He managed to say, "Keep me in the loop, Dr. Martone."

"I will, Jake. And call me Michael."

For the second time that evening, Jake walked out the door, choking on his feelings. The first time he had been angry. Now he was enveloped in fear.

It was 6:45 the next morning and Maddy was at work fifteen minutes ahead of time. She always was. She printed off the updated patient summaries and located the tape recorder for the change of shift report. Although she was younger than the other nurses who worked her shift, she was the charge nurse. That was because she had a master's degree in nursing, and besides, no one else really wanted the position. The extra money for being in charge wasn't worth all the added responsibilities.

Maddy worked on an orthopedic unit. It hadn't been her first choice when she started nursing school. She had set her sights on labor and delivery; she wanted to be part of the joy that a newborn brings to a couple. Her clinical practice in school changed all that. Maybe it was just the patients assigned her during her short training-rotation in obstetrics. But of the six mothers, half were married and only one of those couples seemed really excited about welcoming a child into the world. Of the three single moms, two were no longer in touch with the baby's father. The other one wasn't saying where her boyfriend was; the police were staking the unit just in case he showed. Add to that, Maddy became aware that OB nurses were sued more than any other and were instructed to carry their own liability insurance. It seemed that parents always expected perfect babies and if there were any problems, everyone involved was expected to pay.

Her orthopedic rotation had been revealing in a different way. Most of the patients were on the unit for hip or knee replacements and most of them were elderly and overweight. For many, it had been the extra weight on their joints that necessitated the surgery. It was Maddy's observation that the regular nurses who worked the floor resented their overweight patients and treated them accordingly. It was also true that these patients often had other weight-related problems such as diabetes or kidney failure and that meant more work for the nurses. Also these patients were difficult to move and yet they had to be moved with great precision so as not to undo the work of the surgeon.

Maddy scrutinized all of this and made up her mind that she could make a difference in these people's lives. And, now that she was charge nurse on an orthopedic unit, she did. Everyone who worked on her shift knew what she expected. They also knew that she worked harder than any of them and would be right there to help in the most difficult situations.

When she wasn't involved in direct patient care, she was tackling the enormity of assessment and charting. The fact that it was no longer paper work but computerized hadn't really made things easier. The reality was that the computer had stretched, practically to infinity, all the facets in which a patient could be assessed and that had to be done every eight hours, sometimes every four. When Maddy was at work, her mind was on her work.

That afternoon, as she drove away from the hospital to pick up Emily at school, Maddy's mind turned to Jake and the state of their marriage. Neither was doing well. Last night he had been as non-communicative as ever but there was something different in the way he was shut down. He was sadder, more lost. He hadn't hurled any raw comments her way; Maddy had made up her mind that she wasn't going to tolerate any more of those. But she was worried about him, and worried about them.

Maddy was still in love with Jake and she knew that. She found her mind drifting back to the first time she had met him. She had been awarded a scholarship to Northwestern University to get her MSN. Maddy had never spent more than a week or two out of California, and Chicago was a pleasant surprise. She found Chicago to be very cosmopolitan and was enjoying the adventure. A new friend, Allison, a Chicago native and fellow student, took Maddy under her wing. On a Saturday night, she had brought her to an Old Town bar to check out the singles scene. As in California, the guys were on the make. What was different was that few of them had that posing posture about them; they just seemed to be themselves. One exception was Jonathon. Actually, he wasn't so much posing, as he was just so handsome that he was used to the attention. While girls were catching his eye, he was chatting with the guy next to him. That guy was Jake.

By the ironic look on his face, Jake seemed to enjoy watching his buddy in action, or lack of action; it all seemed to be coming to him. Maddy, sitting at a table halfway across the room, took notice, but it was Jake who had caught her attention. As she was studying the situation, Jake turned and looked in her direction. Had he looked directly at her? Maddy didn't know; his gaze came and went so quickly. Maddy, too, turned away in the manner you do when you don't want someone to know you've been looking at them. But a few seconds later, her eyes returned in his direction. This time, with his head tucked slightly down, his body made a concerted turn in her direction. His face came up, his eyes caught her's. A smile emerged, shaped with just the slightest raising of his thick eyebrows and his upper lip. He held his gaze. Maddy smiled back, a broad, welcoming smile. That smile could have meant a lot of things, but in Maddy's case, it signaled that she wasn't a game player. Jake rose and came toward the table where she and Allison were sitting. He had found an empty chair and pulled it along the way.

"My name is Jake. Do you mind if I join you?"

"I'm Maddy and this is my friend, Allison."

Then it appeared that Jake didn't know what to say next. The three sat with dumb smiles until Jake asked, "Could I get you some fresh beers?"

Allison replied, "Yeah, I'd like that." Maddy smiled and shook her head no. As soon as Jake departed, Allison said, "I might as well get something out of this. His eyes were on you all the while he was coming to our table. Do you want me to disappear in a few minutes?"

"If you don't mind too much. The truth is, he caught me looking at him while he was still at the bar. Something's intriguing about him."

"I don't know about intriguing, but he's a hunk, I'll give him that. I'll spot someone I think I know in about five minutes and get up and leave." She paused briefly and continued, "Don't worry, I can find my own way home."

"Oh, I don't want him to take me home. Unless you find yourself preferring another arrangement, let's reconnect at 12:30 and leave together."

Allison's eyebrows rose urbanely as she replied, "Okay, if that's the way you want it."

Jake soon returned to the table, and after a few minutes, Allison disappeared. Jake appeared more at ease but there was still a little nervousness about him that Maddy found appealing. He asked, "So, do you live here on the Near North?"

"No, I'm up near Evanston. How about you?"

"I'm in Buckstown, so not too far from here."

Maddy inferred that living in Buckstown was supposed to mean something so she said, "I don't know Chicago; I'm from California and have just been here a few weeks. I came out to go to school."

"Northwestern?"

"Yes, a master's nursing program. How'd you know it was Northwestern?"

"Because you mentioned Evanston. You must be smart. That's a tough school to get in," Jake replied.

Maddy just smiled and then changed the subject. "So, what's Buckstown? A neighborhood?"

"Yeah, it's known for being kind of bohemian. It usually impresses girls when I tell them but it didn't get any mileage with you," Jake said with his slow grin surfacing.

Maddy smiled back, "So, are you some kind of bohemian?"

"No, the rent is cheap for being so close to the Loop. I share a good size apartment with my friend Jonathon; he's the guy I was standing next to at the bar." Jake's body language took a sudden turn. Looking restless, he asked, "Do you want to get out of here?"

Maddy thought to herself, "This guy works a little too fast." She replied, "Allison and I are going to leave here together."

"What I mean is, do you want to take a walk? We can be back in forty-five minutes; I promise."

Maddy recalled that there were lots of people on the streets as they came in. She could also sense the restlessness in Jake and identified with it. She really didn't like bars. "Okay, let's go. But, let me find Allison first and tell her."

The two emerged onto Segwick. It was one of those perfect September nights, still possessing the warmth of summer but with early fall dryness permeating the breeze off the lake. Maddy observed Jake. She construed that he was more himself being outside, more himself being in motion. His attempts to engage her in conversation related to asking her about her life in California, what her impressions were of Chicago, and telling her a little about his job selling time for a radio station. But it was what he communicated non-verbally that tantalized Maddy. Maddy loved the way that he would glance at her and then look ahead with an expression that broadcasted that he was the luckiest guy in the world just to be walking down the street with her. She could feel the physicality of his nearness, something primal: bundles of energy just barely being contained. Maddy knew that she would be seeing a lot of this guy and she knew that he knew. She wished that she hadn't arranged things so that she would be leaving with Allison. She knew where she and Jake were heading and no longer saw any reason to delay it.

"Let's go back to the bar. I want to tell Allison that you're taking me home."

The expression on Jake's face was ebullient, not triumphant, but ebullient, like Maddy was opening a hitherto secret door that he had never entered. As for Maddy, she had taken her time easing into her two previous relationships. That wasn't going to work with Jake nor did she want it to.

Maddy spoke to Allison at the bar and as they were walking toward Jake's car, he asked, "Where do you live in Evanston?"

Maddy, who was living in a graduate dorm with a roommate, replied, "Why don't you show me what's so hot about Buckstown?" Jake, already holding her hand, gave it a squeeze.

They had to climb four floors to get to Jake's apartment. The large living room was furnished in guy fashion with two sofas and one TV. Sports magazines lay about on the floor. Jake did not waste time. He guided Maddy right through it and into his bedroom, much neater by contrast. If Jake had seemed boyish and unsure of himself, he was all confidence as he undressed Maddy and then himself. He made love to her in such a masterful way that Maddy felt like it was the first time that she had been with a man. Really a man. All Jake's bound-up energy that she had sensed earlier was being released, and yet, it was all about her. He truly was making love; it wasn't a euphemistic expression.

After that night, Jake engaged Maddy in a whirlwind courtship: sailing on the lake, the end-of-season outdoor concerts, bicycle rides that ended with a picnic which he prepared (more accurately, had a deli prepare), every romantic venture Jake could think of. One Saturday afternoon, they went to the driving range at Lincoln Park, basically for her to watch Jake's expertise at hitting the ball. Maddy thought it was cute; it reminded her of the courtship rituals in nature movies when the male makes a display of his prowess.

Jake had started saying, "I love you" during the first week. He later told Maddy that he wanted to say it that first night but he didn't want to scare her. By the end of the second month, during a blustery November evening carriage ride down Michigan Avenue, he proposed. Maddy accepted; she had never been so sure about anything. Her one condition was that they'd wait until the following summer.

After several months passed, and Jake had made no effort to introduce her to his mother, Maddy asked to meet her. They were invited a couple weeks later to dinner at the home where Jake had grown up. For three people, and considering that two of them were mother and son, the evening was surprisingly formal. Maddy hypothesized that this was the difference between Chicago and the more casual L.A.

Maddy's thoughts were jarred from Chicago memories to present day California when she saw Emily approaching her car. Jake was right; she was the image of herself. In recent months, Maddy had been feeling that her family consisted of just Emily and herself. What frightened her at this instant was how used she was becoming to that idea.

Chapter 8: Emotional Lockdown

Emily had a dance recital the following evening. Of all the girls in her dance class, Emily was the most sophisticated. Emily preferred wearing her thick blonde hair long and brushed away from her face. It was held by a band of matching color to whatever she was wearing. She didn't have her mom's defining cheek bones, they would possibly emerge in time, but she did have her green eyes.

Seven-year-old Emily did look like her mom. But Emily was more complicated and had been from the start. As a baby, she had been hypersensitive; if you were pushing her in her stroller and went over a sidewalk crack a little too roughly, she took it as a personal insult. At age two, she had decidedly definite ideas. There was a six-month period when she would only wear a dress and a dress of her choosing. Maddy was surprised that she would tolerate such behavior, but as most young parents discover, having a child is a humbling experience. Some children need more love and Emily was one of them. Fortunately for her, both her parents understood.

All the girls at the recital wore pink leotards, Emily would have preferred black but this decision really was out of her control. What she did control was how precise she was with her dance movements. She was so much more advanced than the others that the teacher decided to put her front and center. Emily's precision wasn't driven by a desire to outshine the others, but like both her parents, what she did, she did well.

The small studio, housed in a storefront, was neatly painted white with a small stage and folding chairs arranged theater-style. Recorded music came through a sound system, primitive by L.A. standards, but the focus of the audience would be on the performers. Maddy and Jake, Maddy's sister Colleen, and their mother, Robin, were included in the audience.

As the lights went down and the music came up, ten fledgling dancers appeared from stage left. After circling the stage twice, the girls, a few of them needing to first see where others landed, found their positions. Emily had gracefully glided to center stage. No one in her family had known that she was going to be featured, and Jake had an uncharacteristic, almost goofy, broad grin on his face. He was so proud of his little girl. Maddy came first in his life, but he loved Emily intensely. He never had a sister, never had friends who were girls, and Emily was one amazing mystery to him. Although he never shared the sentiment with Maddy, when they were expecting, he had wanted a son whom he could name after his father. They chose to wait until the baby was born before knowing the sex, and from her first second in this world, Jake was mesmerized, hooked. Once in anger, he had accused Maddy of trying to create in Emily a replica of herself. But he knew as everyone in the family knew, that although she looked like Maddy, she was Jake incarnate.

The second number of the short program called for a costume change. Soon the girls returned to the stage dressed as cowgirls, riding hobbyhorses to the tune of an old Gene Autry song. This time Emily mixed in with all the rest but her gallop was the most defined and in sync with the music. If she realized that she was better than the rest, you couldn't tell it. Her face only showed her concentration on what she was doing.

After the recital, they all went out to eat at a restaurant that had a sign proclaiming, "Serving the Valley since 1946," and was known for their homemade chicken pot pies. Jake was playing host, engaging Maggie's mother and sister in light conversation and bringing the topic back to Emily's performance with regularity. Each time it produced a quiet smile on Emily's face. Jake loved seeing his little girl smile.

Maddy, too, was smiling, smiling with contentment. Here were the people she loved most in the world, all together, enjoying each other's company. It had been a while since she had seen Jake this happy and relaxed. Well, not really relaxed, but relaxed for Jake.

When they arrived home, and after still more accolades for the performer, both parents put Emily to bed. Then, as they exited her room,

Jake took Maddy in his arms and kissed her. The electricity was still there, with Jake it was always there. He then followed his familiar ritual of leading Maddy into the bedroom where he made love to her. During these sexual interludes, Maddy had the gift of always being in the present, giving back to Jake what he was giving to her. But, later that night, after Jake had fallen asleep, Maddy replayed their love-making in her mind. Something in the last few years had changed. What was it? Jake was still as tender. But, what was it? Was it something about Jake himself? "Yes," she thought, "But what?" Then it came to her, more as a feeling than as an idea. A hint of desperation had crept in and it was intensifying. Maddy felt that Jake had some desperate need to connect with life itself and sex seemed to be his only avenue. It alarmed Maddy a bit, and her early evening contentment faded.

Jake had never taken the initiative to invite Uncle Frank over for dinner, and the following morning, Maddy decided to take the matter in hand. When Jake returned from the driving range, she approached the subject. "Why don't you call your Uncle Frank and see if he could come to dinner? See if he has plans for this evening, or tomorrow evening." Jake didn't make eye contact and Maddy wondered if he had heard her. "Jake, did you hear me? Why don't you invite your uncle over?"

Jake replied tersely, "I don't think that would be a good idea right now," hoping that would end the subject but knowing better; Maddy never allowed herself to be blown off.

"Why's that, Jake?"

"He's not feeling real good, right now."

"Have you talked to him? What's wrong with him?"

"Yeah, I talked with him on Thursday. He's in the hospital. St. John's in Santa Monica."

"Jake, what's wrong with him? Why do I have to pull this out of you?"

Jake hardly knew the answer to that himself. Since the topic of his going for counseling arose, he had pretty much decided he didn't want the two of them to meet, at least until that storm had passed. Even after he knew that Frank was sick, he still felt that they'd gang up on him and, in his gut, he knew he couldn't stand the pressure. He was just getting through a difficult transition into a new job, a job he didn't like. He was getting through the best he could, putting his head down and plowing through.

"What's wrong with your uncle, Jake?" Maddy asked, once again, in a calm but firm voice.

"He has Non-Hodgkin's lymphoma."

"How long have you known?"

"I just found out about it a few days ago."

"And you didn't want to tell me about it? Why, for God's sake?" Jake just looked at her, not knowing what to say.

"What are you afraid of, Jake? Am I that threatening that you can't tell me that your uncle's been given a serious diagnosis? What did you think I was going to say? What did you think that I was going to do? I don't understand, Jake."

"I can't explain it," replied Jake, followed by a long silence.

"That's not good enough, Jake. You're a grown man. You should know why you do things." Again, there was an uneasy silence. "Jake, I'm not going to tolerate your refusal to communicate. I've told you that before and you know me well enough that I mean what I say."

Jake was feeling cornered. "He has Non-Hodgkin's lymphoma. Now I've told you, okay."

"Jake, I'm sorry that your uncle is sick, but it isn't about that anymore. It's the fact that you couldn't tell me about it. That's not right."

"Okay, I wish I had told you. Let's get off this? Okay."

"No, Jake, it's not okay. This is why we need to go to couple's counseling to find out how we can communicate better."

"Damn it. I knew this is where you were going to take it. You know how I feel about that. I'm not going to do it."

"Jake, I'm not going to ask you again."

"Is that some kind of threat?"

"I mean it, Jake."

"Good, then that's the last goddamn time I'll ever have to hear you talk about it." Jake walked out of the house. He didn't storm out in anger. Rather, he was out of ammunition and he knew it. It always happened that way with Maddy. She didn't play games and you couldn't trip her into one.

Jake went back to the driving range, but he couldn't get the look on Maddy's face off his mind. It scared him. Scared him in a way he hadn't felt since he was a little boy. He had to do something; yellow gladiolas had always worked before.

After driving downtown to the flower mart, Jake returned home. He walked in with his peace offering in hand. Maddy was in the kitchen, but rather than reaching for the flowers as she had done in the past, she stood motionless, looking at him.

Jake froze. "These aren't easy to find this time of year," he uttered softly.

"It's no good, Jake. I'm leaving you."

Jake was stunned. The world that he knew was totally sucked out of him, replaced with an emptiness that seared through every cell of his body. He felt woozy. He wanted to put the flowers down but couldn't. Jake started to say something, but had a hard time finding his voice. Finally, he replied, "Maddy, you know I love you more than anything else in the world. Don't do this. Please, don't do this."

Jake was breaking Maddy's heart. She saw a pleading little boy whom she wanted to take into her arms and comfort. But they had been through this before. It had never come to this point, but how many times had she reached out to Jake, only to be shut out the next day. Or if not, the next week. She wanted a marriage and this wasn't measuring up. Maybe her mother could put up with it for a lifetime; she would not.

Maddy felt the need to add, "Colleen came over and picked up Emily. I didn't want her here while we had this discussion."

A new horror possessed Jake as he realized that Emily wouldn't be in his life every day. Reading his mind, Maddy continued, "Jake, you're a terrific father. I'll tell you right now that I'll agree to joint custody. Don't worry about that."

"Don't do this, Maddy," Jake repeated.

But, Maddy noted he wasn't saying, "Let's go get some counseling and work this out." If he had, she would have relented. Instead, she simply stated. "Jake, I told you that I meant it and I do."

She could have left a note but she respected and loved Jake too much not to tell him face to face. It was the hardest thing that Maddy ever had to do. Her own heart breaking, she walked toward him, kissed him lightly on his check, and then walked out. Jake was still holding the gladiolas as he heard her car pull away.

Jake didn't know what to do. He knew he had to get away from there; everywhere he looked he saw Maddy and Emily and their life together. It was as if a giant cleaver had severed him from everything that meant anything. He got into his car and started driving without a destination. Feelings were coming at him in waves and they were all horrific. It was as though the electricity that comes with good sex had turned to its dark side and was now running through his body at will. With the passing of time, the torment only worsened. Pain that had been tucked away since childhood was now seeping through. Hungry devils unleashed. Stopped at a traffic light, Jake put his head on the steering wheel and screamed. Other drivers looked over at him but in Southern California, frustrations run rampant, and they paid little heed. The next light he actually drove through on red, narrowly missing crosstraffic. Shaken up all the more, he knew he had to stop driving and go somewhere. But where? He knew that the driving range couldn't distract him. Not this time.

Uncle Frank came into his mind. How he wished that Frank wasn't sick and in the hospital. He had to talk to someone and Uncle Frank was the only one he could think of. He had programmed Dr. Martone's cell number into his phone and punched out the number. Doing his best to steady his voice, he said, "Dr. Martone, this is Jake Ford. I was wondering if this might be a good time for me to stop by St. John's and see my uncle."

Michael detected the urgency in Jake's voice and weighed his decision. He didn't want Frank to be burdened, but also knew how Frank felt about Jake and what he would want. "Sure Jake, this would be a good time. He's through with his treatment for today. He's on the second floor, room 234. Be prepared for isolation procedures; the nurse will explain them to you before you enter his room."

"Thanks, Dr. Martone."

Michael added, "Jake, chemotherapy takes a lot out of you. Don't stay more than twenty minutes. And stop calling me Dr. Martone. It's Michael, remember?"

"Okay, thanks, Michael," Jake said hurriedly, hoping not to betray the desperation he was feeling.

It took him 30 minutes to get to St. John's. When he approached room 234, he saw a sign saying, "Isolation: Report to the nursing station." There, he was instructed that before entering his uncle's room, he was to wash his hands carefully with sanitizer and put on a yellow gown and facemask. The nurse explained that the chemotherapy treatment was destroying so many of his uncle's white blood cells that he had little natural immunity to fight infection.

Jake did as he was instructed and entered the room. Frank appeared to be dozing so Jake just sat down and already felt a bit better just being with his uncle. Frank, sensing that someone was in the room, opened his eyes. "Hello, Jake," he said groggily. "This is a nice surprise."

"I called Michael and he said that it was okay to stop by."

"Of course," replied Frank, now fully awake. Taking a more focused view of his nephew, and sensing that something was wrong, he asked, "Jake, what's going on? I can see that you're troubled."

Jake appreciated the fact that he didn't have to attempt chitchat; he wasn't together enough to manage it. He replied, "Maddy's left me." It cut right through him just to say it.

"Jake, oh Jake, I'm so sorry," responded Frank with deep sincerity. "I can't imagine how painful this must be for you."

"It's pretty bad."

"When did this happen?"

"Just today. Just a little while ago."

"I'm glad that you came here, Jake. I don't know what I can say that can comfort you, but I'm glad that you came. I wish that I could just absorb some of your pain so that you don't have to carry it all yourself."

"Uncle Frank, you're the only person I could think to turn to. Pretty pathetic, isn't it?"

"No, Jake, it's not. We're family, you and I. I know that I haven't been there for much of your life; let me be a real uncle now. There's nothing that I wouldn't do for you, please know that." There was a short pause and Frank asked, "Where are you going to live?"

"Haven't thought that far."

"Come stay at my house. It's large enough that we wouldn't be getting in each other's way. It would mean a lot to me if you would. There's plenty of room for Emily, too. Please consider it."

"Wow, Uncle Frank. Are you sure?"

"If you're worried that I'm too sick to have someone there, think again. You could run errands for me, help me out in all kind of ways."

"I am good at handyman kind of stuff."

"I never have been, so that's great." After a brief pause, Frank continued, "Jake, I've already thought of something that you can get me. I've never worn baseball caps but my hair's starting to fall out from the chemo so now I have a reason to. Can you pick up a couple? I don't care what insignia they have."

"Why not the Cubs and the Bears? It's your old hometown."

"I like that idea." A silence fell before Frank resumed, "Jake, ever notice the rock garden in my back yard?"

"Yeah."

"The large red rock is fake; you'll find a key box underneath. Move in anytime, the sooner the better as far as I'm concerned. I'll be in here a couple more weeks and I like the idea of someone being in the house."

The two visited for another 10 minutes. Most of that time, Frank managed to distract Jake from his crisis, giving him a short respite. Jake, meanwhile, kept in mind Michael's admonition to keep his visit short. When Jake stood and said that he had to go, Frank interjected, "Jake, you know me. I can't pass up an opportunity to pass out some unsolicited advice. Hold onto this: right now, you've been given a pretty good wallop, about as bad as it gets. Be easy on yourself. Getting through each hour and each day is a big accomplishment right now. Give yourself lots of credit for just doing that."

"Thanks," replied Jake as he turned to leave.

"Oh, and one more thing. I know you can't believe this, but it's really true. Just as these blasts that try to mow you down come at you in life, there's all kinds of good things that come your way that you don't anticipate. Most people don't think about that, but it's true."

Jake looked at his uncle and then smiled for the first time that day. "I do believe it, Uncle Frank. It just happened when you invited me to stay with you."

Chapter 9: Frank's Special Place

Frank remained in the hospital another three weeks. An infection set in at the nadir of his treatment that had required close monitoring. Meanwhile, Jake had moved into one of Frank's guest rooms. He took only his clothes with him, part of him wanting Maddy to have anything that she might need, part of him still hoping that he'd be moving back home again. Jake got in touch with Michael on a daily basis, wanting to know if it was a good idea to visit Frank and at what time. He liked Michael. There was a growing friendship between them built around their sincere affection for Frank.

Frank was discharged on a Wednesday afternoon and Jake had arranged his schedule to be at the hospital to take him home. Frank was scheduled to return in a week to start the next round of chemotherapy; his form of lymphoma was proving to be disturbingly aggressive. Jake listened to the nurse's discharge instructions; he wanted to know everything he needed to do to care for his uncle. But he also knew Michael would be around often enough to answer any questions.

One such question arose on Saturday morning. Frank was restless from his hospital stay and was eager for a seaside outing. Unbeknown to Frank, Jake made a hurried call to clear the idea with Michael. Permission was granted. Jake returned to the kitchen where Frank, wearing a Cubs cap, was finishing his breakfast. Jake interjected, "I'm not picking up Emily until early this evening so we have all day ahead of us. Anywhere you want to go is fine with me."

"There's a place at Sunrise Beach. Have you been to Sunrise Beach?"

"I know where it is."

"I bet you don't know the place I'm talking about. It's a bit remote. You have to hike over some big rocks to get there." Frank could see a look of apprehension cross Jake's face. "Don't worry about it. We'll take our time. If I need to stop every couple of minutes to rest, I will."

"Are you sure that's what you want to be doing right now. You've only been home two days."

"Jake, it really is what I want to do. It would mean a lot to me."

Jake replied, "I've got an idea. Why don't you lie down for a bit after you finish eating and rest? While you're doing that, I'll run over to the grocery and pick up some picnic stuff from their deli section."

"That sounds great. I've had picnics at this spot before."

"Anything from the grocery sound good to you?"

Frank hadn't really had an appetite in months but he smiled and replied, "If they have some decadent brownies, the chewy kind, I'd like that."

Jake responded, "Sounds good to me." But in truth he hadn't really regained his appetite since the split with Maddy.

The two left Sherman Oaks around 10:30 and found their way to the San Diego Freeway heading south. Weekend traffic wasn't bad, but bad is always a relative term when it comes to Southern California freeways. Frank seemed to be vitalized by the drive, a welcome change from the seriousness of a hospital room that had been made more somber by isolation procedures. Sensing this, Jake left him alone with his thoughts.

After crossing into Orange County, they turned toward the coast, and with Frank giving specific directions, they arrived in a parking lot not far from the beach. All around them were surfers changing out of wet suits, a common sight in this lot because topography of the coast nearby produced favorable waves. Jake reached for the tote bag and picnic basket and Frank did not challenge Jake's unspoken decision to carry both.

After they descended a long set of stairs leading down to the beach, Frank sat down on the final landing to catch his breath. With alarm in his voice, Jake asked, "Are you sure you want to go on, Uncle Frank? We could have our picnic right here as far as I'm concerned. The ocean's beautiful from right here."

"Just give me a moment, Jake. All these weeks in the hospital, I've wanted to come to my special spot. We're so close now. We just have to walk across the beach to the north. Then see those rocks? We have to climb across a few of those. That's all."

"Whatever you want, Uncle Frank. Anytime you want to rest, let me know and I'll put one of these towels down for you."

"Thanks, Jake. I'm rested now. Let's go."

Frank made it across the beach and started climbing across the big rocks before he needed to stop again. Climbing on the rocks was hard on him. He was not only fatigued but it was obvious that he was in pain and it was tough for Jake to see his uncle's physical capacity so reduced. After a few more rests, they arrived at Frank's special place.

It was a point where they could go no further. They stood on a precipice overlooking a cove. The blue Pacific was crashing against a wall of rock below and the spray from the ongoing impact drifted upwards and kissed their cheeks. When the waves pulled back, the water, green and blue and white, churned into a kaleidoscope of shapes and hues. Overhead, seagulls cruised against a cloudless blue sky, looking for food, their honking song blending with the sound of the waves. There was a commanding fragrance of the sea, fish, salt and seaweed all combined. One's senses were bombarded on every level, yet this was a place of peace because all was in harmony. Man could not orchestrate anything with such completeness.

The two men stood in silence for several moments. Then Jake removed a blanket from the tote and spread it on a rock so that his uncle could sit. Jake sat down next to him. Frank broke through the human stillness and uttered, "It's something, isn't it?"

"Sure is, Uncle Frank. I can't believe that we're the only ones here."

"Sometimes, there's a fisherman or two. But most people aren't willing to climb over these rocks to see what's on the other side."

"That sounds like one of your life lessons, Uncle Frank," Jake said with a smile.

Frank replied, "It does, doesn't it? Jake, I hope you don't find all my observations too tedious."

"I don't, Uncle Frank," Jake replied with newfound genuineness. He wanted to say that he knew that all the advice given was because Frank loved him, but those were words that he couldn't get out of his mouth. He just couldn't. Instead, he found himself changing the subject. "How did you find this place, anyway?"

"I'd like to say that I saw the rocks and decided to climb them to see what was on the other side. But to be honest, someone else introduced me to this spot."

"Was that a long time ago?"

"Let me think. I'd say about seventeen years ago."

"And, you've been coming here ever since?"

"The truth is that I haven't been here in seven years." Frank could tell that Jake was curious as to why he hadn't returned in such a long time, but was bowing to discretion not to ask. Frank continued, "There's a part of my life that we haven't talked about, Jake." Jake looked at his uncle in such a way as to say that he was receptive to hear whatever his uncle wanted to reveal.

Frank continued, "I know that you know I'm gay even though we haven't discussed it. And I was proud when you weren't afraid to tread onto the gay terrain when you told me about Ty Moran. That took some courage, considering.

"Now I do feel like talking about it. I had a partner for ten years named Eddie. He's the one who first brought me here. He grew up nearby. I had had other relationships before Eddie, but when he came into my life, I decided to love him with my whole heart, no holding back. I don't know if that was because he was the person he was, or because I was at a point in my life to do so. Probably some of both. Anyway, I did, and it was wonderful. I loved the steadiness about him; he always seemed to try to do the right thing. He laughed at my attempts at humor so, of course, I thought he had a wonderful sense of humor. I was happy just to be with him and he seemed happy to be with me. Those ordinary little moments I keep talking about, going to the grocery with him, working together in the yard, it all seemed extraordinary to me. It was the happiest ten years of my life."

Frank looked over at his nephew who had been listening intently. He said, "I know what you're wondering: 'What happened to bring an end to Shangri-La?' Jake, whoever knows exactly what happens in these matters? Eddie was an aeronautical engineer, working in a huge office in Redondo Beach. His work schedule was predictable, much like his dad's had been during his boyhood years. My schedule was much more fluid with evening events bleeding in with the work I did during the day. Also, Eddie was uncomfortable mixing with famous people. I think over the years he started yearning for a more regular life.

"Furthermore, Eddie was twelve years younger than I. When we first met, he was so convinced that it didn't matter that I was equally convinced. But, in time, it did matter. By the time he reached his early forties, I think he hit a midlife crisis and felt that life was passing him by. One day before he went to work, he told me that he was unhappy and had been for some time and that he was leaving me. And then he did. He walked out the door and that was that. The following weekend he was back to pick up his things and made it clear that there was no room for negotiation. His decision was irrevocable."

"You haven't seen him since?"

"I ran into him one time. That was maybe five years ago. He and his new friend were at an ice cream parlor on Santa Monica Boulevard. We exchanged pleasantries. That was it."

"How did that make you feel?"

"I knew about the new partner. Eddie was in another relationship within a matter of months and a mutual friend had let me know. And, yes, the guy was younger; he looked to be about the same age as Eddie. To be honest with you, Jake, it was a jarring experience, even though several years had gone by. It was my ego that was crushed. As soon as I heard that he was with someone new, I was convinced that he could never be as happy with that person as he had been with me. And in a matter of time, he'd realize that. But, seeing the two of them together, they seemed happy enough. He had moved on."

Jake couldn't help but identify, his own wounds being so fresh. It had never dawned on him that Frank might have had a similar experience. It made more sense now, why Frank responded so quickly that afternoon in the hospital, insisting that he move in with him.

Jake set up the picnic food on the blanket, and the two men sat, looking into the cove, both lost in their thoughts. After several moments, Frank's stream of consciousness became verbal. "I'm just realizing something about myself, something that has been in front of my nose, so close, that I didn't see it. I've been thinking, Jake, why, in all this time, I had never mentioned to you that I was gay. I think that I've been telling myself for years that I'm discreet by nature. Well, I guess I am discreet by nature. But underneath all the self-talk that I'm comfortable with my sexuality, I think I've held onto a residue of shame.

"I think my earliest image of a homosexual was some pervert lurking in a public park, looking for innocent prey. The idea repulsed me and, God knows, the possibility that I might be one repulsed me even more. Thank God times changed and I began to realize that perfectly decent people, people that I enjoyed being with, were attracted to their own sex physically and romantically. In my lifetime, homosexuality has gone from being one of the psychiatric mental health diagnoses to the ordination of gay ministers in mainstream churches. I've hardly been a vanguard in the movement for enlightenment on this issue. I've been one of the fortunate recipients that had to be dragged along. Living here in Southern California made that easier for me."

Frank drifted back into silence. Jake was remembering his mother's ramblings about perverts when he was a child. And he remembered the boys in school who were suspected of being gay, and how being called "fag" was the ultimate insult. He looked toward his uncle and simply replied, "I'm glad times have changed, Uncle Frank."

Frank smiled and said, "Thanks, Jake. Me too."

The two men, cast in a spell by the sights and sounds about them, ate their lunch slowly, comfortable in each other's presence, not needing to engage in idle conversation. A good hour elapsed. Finally Frank suggested that it was time to go. Jake could see that his uncle was fatigued, but he also understood that it had been worthwhile for him to climb across the rocks; this destination had served as a pilgrimage.

 After a number of rests, two just getting up the stairs to the parking lot, they found their car and drove home. Frank went immediately to bed and an hour later, Jake drove to Studio City to pick up Emily. Jake hated the moment of turning into the driveway, knowing now that it wasn't his home any longer. He hated that he had to ring the bell. But, most of all, he hated the fact that Maddy now came to the door, smiled and welcomed him, but welcomed him as an outsider. How did Frank express it? "Eddie had moved on." Well, it was clear that Maddy was moving on as well.

"Hi, Jake. Come in. Emily's just getting her things. She's ready."

"How are you doing, Maddy?"

"Fine, Jake. How about you?"

"I'm fine," replied Jake, in total contradiction to his feelings.

"Jake, before Emily comes out, I want to tell you that you'll hear from my lawyer in a few days; he'll be sending some papers."

Jake was speechless. He wanted to beg her to slow things down, but the part of him that wouldn't /couldn't participate in any kind of therapy was intransigent. It didn't make any sense, even to him; it was as if he had an internal lock for which there was no key. He just stood there looking at Maddy, the lost little boy that she had seen so often. He was breaking her heart.

Finally, Emily emerged. Jake extended his arms to give her a hug and Emily complied, albeit a bit stiffly. It wasn't that she didn't want a hug from her father, but for Emily this new arrangement with her daddy living away from home was a difficult adjustment. Both Maddy and Jake read their daughter's body language and both felt anguish.

"You're sure my beautiful girl," Jake interjected.

With that, Maddy bent down to kiss her daughter's cheek and said, "See you tomorrow night, cutie. Enjoy your time with Daddy. Jake, try to get her back by 8:00 so she gets a good night's sleep before school on Monday."

"I will," he replied, and Maddy knew that she could bank on it.

So went another painful encounter of seeing Maddy but not being with her. They drove back to Uncle Frank's and Frank was still sleeping. The two of them changed into swimsuits and met at the pool. Emily had swimming lessons the year before and was competent in the water. They played a game throwing a ball, and as both of them were diving here and there, Jake heard his daughter laugh for the first time since he left home. He broke out in a big smile and started exaggerating his moves clownishly and she laughed all the harder.

Jake was so glad that he could bring Emily to Frank's house. He remembered being in the various Marine World Parks and seeing fathers alone with their children. Advertising claims of, "The happiest day ever," weren't evident on their faces. Instead, they looked helpless, as if they were looking for something that just wasn't there. Now Jake understood why. Uncle Frank was right about his mantra of the small ordinary moments being the most extraordinary. What he missed most of Emily was just watching her walk through the room, seeing her schoolbooks on the kitchen table, knowing that she was there and that he was there too. At least at Frank's, they could have some of that.

Jake told Emily he'd need her to help him with his work the following morning. The next day they were off to a remote broadcast held at the opening of a new car dealership. The destination was Van Nuys so at least they didn't have to travel far. From Jake's point of view, there really wasn't any reason for him to be there. He had already handled everything on his end and the technical people would be there to manage everything else. What he really didn't like about remotes, a situation in which the broadcast originates from outside the studio, was the "Yeah, rah, let's put on a show" attitude. Jake wasn't very good at "Yeah, rah." Both the client and the radio station personnel acted like something momentously important was going on. And, of course, Ben and Jay expected that kind of energy when they deigned to meet their humdrum public. Jake and Emily helped hand out some coffee and donuts. All the while, Jake looked for the first chance for escape, which they took expeditiously.

Later in the afternoon, Jake and Frank were sitting on the patio while Emily sat nearby, dutifully doing her homework. Emily had liked Frank on their first meeting; he had seen to that.

Jake was lamenting about the morning experience. "I never like being around Ben and Jay, but they were particularly unbearable this morning."

"Why's that?"

"Remember telling me about the ego thing, something about raw ego being sickening?"

"Yeah, I do. Is that what you saw going on?"

"In the worst way. They were so phony with the people; I know they hated being there, but I also saw how they ate all the adoration up. It's foul."

"I've seen what you're talking about. It's all the more desperate when people are on the downslide of fame. From what you've told me about the station's trajectory, it sounds like that's what's going on."

"Exactly."

"Jake, what is it that you would really want to do? I mean, if money were no object, and you could change careers in midstream, what would you want to do? Don't think about it. Just tell me the first thing that pops into your mind."

Jake blurted out, "I'd like to teach history, World History, on the college level."

"Then why not do it?"

"I veered off of that course a long time ago. I don't see how I can get back on."

"Think about it," was all that Frank said.

The doorbell rang. Jake started to get up but Frank said, "It's Michael. He's just ringing the bell as a formality; he'll find us back here." Michael did. He brought with him some deli salad and dessert, and Jake turned his mind to cooking on the grill.

Chapter 10: Journey into Darkness

The following Thursday, Jake took his uncle back to St. John's. After Frank was settled, Jake departed the hospital and drove east toward the 405 Freeway. His plan was to return to Frank's, but as he drove, he started thinking about Maddy and the previous weekend. Sunday hadn't been any easier than Saturday. In fact, it was rougher because Jake had had a day to think about the fact that Maddy's lawyer would soon be contacting him.

The lawyer's papers arrived on Wednesday. Maddy had proposed selling their home so that they could split the equity 50/50. Jake had put a big X through it and wrote on the bottom that she could have the house. No questions asked. That letter was in his briefcase to mail. Maddy was moving on, that's all there was to it, and he was lying down, letting her. He asked himself, "What kind of man am I that I'm letting the woman I love, walk out of my life without a fight?" Then, he found his body freezing, realizing his only option was to get into therapy. "Why can't I do that? People do it all the time."

But, his body continued to tense to the point that he felt like he was choking. "Goddamn, I can't breathe! Goddamn it, what's wrong with me?"

As he approached the freeway, he remembered Frank telling him that he had to go to Chicago to find the answer. He still didn't know what that meant. But he so desperately wanted to be back with Maddy and Emily, that with the same impetuousness with which he had decided to go find his uncle's house for the first time, he now decided to the take the 405 South and head toward LAX. He called his office and reported that he'd be out all day, but would be back in the morning. Jake parked in short-term parking; he wanted to get on a flight as quickly as possible before he lost his courage. Once in the terminal, he headed toward U.S. Trans Airways, a carrier which offered discounted tickets all through the day.

Jake's mother was born Karen Houvash on Chicago's Southside, and grew up in the blue-collar neighborhood of Beverly. Her father, Walt, worked at a nearby paint factory, and also worked a second job as a night watchman at the

Pullman Building. Margaret, her mother, worked at a school cafeteria. Both her parents were gentle creatures and, from their perspective, they had come a long way.

They owned their home, owned a car, owned a TV. Sure, they were making payments on everything, but who wasn't? During one particularly hard stretch, their TV was repossessed, but that had happened to other neighbors as well. All in all, life was good, and they'd often get together with those same neighbors to play cards on weekends.

Karen had extraordinary looks. The adults in the neighborhood often said that she resembled Marilyn Novak. That was before Marilyn left Chicago, dyed her hair platinum, and became film star, Kim Novak. But for Karen, why bother to look like a movie star if only to remain in the old neighborhood. By her mid-teens, Karen developed a disdain for her parents' contentment. Her older brothers didn't escape her judgement either, particularly after they chose to go to work right out of high school.

Karen enrolled in a community college and studied to be an English teacher. She wasn't driven by a desire to teach as much as she wanted the security that tenure in the Chicago Public School system would bring. Karen completed her degree at the four-year campus at DeKalb and set her sights on landing a job north of the Loop.

She was as good as a teacher could be, who didn't have her heart in it. She was well organized, well prepared, and had no problem with discipline in the classroom.

The times were rampant with women demanding equal rights, but girls who came through the community college system generally weren't marching in the street with their more affluent sisters. They relied on more traditional steps to power and Karen was no exception. In a matter of months, Karen met Julie, another young teacher who had grown up in the cosmopolitan neighborhood of Roger's Park. Karen latched onto her when she realized that her new friend had single brothers with professional degrees. She was soon weaving herself into their social network.

She became aware that the Chicago accent north of the Loop didn't have as hard of a flat "a" as the Southside's, and she immediately worked conscientiously to soften hers. Replicating other women in her new social set, she exhibited a newfound charm that featured an easy laugh and a lightness of attitude that belied the steel rigidity that lay beneath.

Karen wasn't so much sexually precocious as she knew how to give men what they wanted, and more. She had been a quick learner. What she really wanted was to be important in the world. Important meant that she'd be noticed. It meant that she'd be respected. It also meant that she'd be feared if need be. And it meant that she'd never be vulnerable. Vulnerability would only get in the way.

In less than a year, she met Jake's father. He didn't know what hit him. Here was a gorgeous brunette who apparently couldn't get enough of him. In no time, he was envisioning their life together. He already had a good position as an engineer, and now he'd have a wife who taught school and would be a wonderful mother to his kids. He wanted lots of kids. He loved his older brother Frank, but they had been so different and he felt that his childhood would have been fuller had the family been larger. In less than a year, they were married. A year later, Jake was born. After a few more years, Tom understood, even if he didn't know it in a way that he could put in words, that happiness wasn't important to Karen. A more primal consideration held precedence.

Karen knew she wasn't much of a wife, at least in the ways that Tom wanted her to be. She didn't understand that she was afraid to love him; she just knew that she couldn't. She tried making up for it by navigating a path where he'd be successful, thinking that someday he'd be grateful. That day never came.

Likewise, Karen wanted to be a good mom. Often, when Jake was a little boy, she wanted to grab him into her arms and hold him for dear life. Something always stopped her: a deep-down, unconscious fear that she might touch a vulnerability that would cause her to unravel. When Jake was a teenager, and she was sure that she could look at him without his knowing, she would study him and be proud.

The first flight that Jake tried to catch was full and the following one wouldn't leave until 11:30 A.M. There were also the complications that he hadn't a reservation and was traveling without luggage. Security found this odd, and Jake had to endure an extensive search and explain why he was flying to Chicago and then returning just a few hours later. He told them the truth that he wanted to make a surprise visit to his mother. They seemed satisfied.

Jake arrived at O'Hare a little before 5:00 P.M. Central time, and took the L to the Northern Loop. His mother had moved from his boyhood home to a residential skyscraper overlooking Lake Michigan. Jake had never been there but knew the address, which indicated that she lived on the 41st floor. He knew how to find her building easy enough, but he was losing his nerve. "What the hell am I doing here? What am I supposed to be asking her? Uncle Frank, you're a great guy, but what the fuck were you talking about?"

All the physical symptoms that had arisen with previous consideration of therapy were now upon him. His body felt tight; he was hyperventilating, his ears were burning, and his thoughts were rushing through his head, none of them welcome. Jake walked toward the lake and could see his mother's building. He crossed Lakeshore Drive and turned in the opposite direction, walking hurriedly for 20 minutes. Then he came to a dead stop. "Maddy and Emily," he said to himself. "They're everything to me. Whatever it takes, I'm going to do this." Jake turned around and walked determinedly toward his mother's building.

Karen's title at Thorton Industries was Vice President of Acquisitions, but her specialty was firing the dead weight, or anyone who she thought was getting paid too much. She didn't have trouble with that undertaking, she would do what the job called for. Karen kept herself very fit and wore clothes purchased on

Chicago's Miracle Mile. However, if the expression, "By fifty, you have the face you deserve," is accurate, then for Karen Ford, it served as an indictment. The classic Slavic features that had defined her youthful beauty had hardened and her eyes spoke of a chronic sadness.

Karen was at home. She was most evenings unless traveling on business. Her apartment looked like something out of a magazine, like a decorator might have put together and, indeed, one had. A visitor, and there were very few, looking about would glean little about the occupant's personal life. The only personal picture within view was that of Karen and Mayor Daley, taken at a fundraiser. Karen had a corner apartment and from the 41st floor, the view of Lake Michigan was magnificent.

For some years now, Karen had a few drinks to relax in the evening and she had had a few tonight. The phone rang. It was the doorman saying that a young man, stating that he was her son, was in the lobby. "What's he look like?" Karen asked in bewilderment.

"Blonde hair, blue eyes, says he lives in California and is in town on business."

"Let me talk to him."

"Hi, Mom. I'm here on a quick business trip. Going back tonight. Had an extra hour before heading to the airport and thought I'd surprise you."

"Jake, what a nice surprise," Karen exclaimed in total truthfulness. For years, she had felt she had lost her son and she now sensed a minute spark of fresh hope. She continued, "Give the phone back to Jerry and I'll tell him to let you up."

It took a few minutes for Jake to arrive at her door, and Karen, wearing a hostess gown, winter sea green in color, was waiting for him on the other side. "Come in," she said with a genuine smile. There were no hugs; there had never been hugs.

"Hi, Mom. You look great. Glad you were home."

"Tomorrow night I wouldn't have been. I'm flying to Rochester, New York, tomorrow. Come in and take a look at this place. Something, isn't it?"

"Sure is, Mom." Jake walked over to the window and looked out toward the lake. It was just transitioning from dusk to night, and he could still see the barges and freighters fading into the darkness of the lake, their blinking lights coming into their own. "Really, Mom, this is some view."

Karen was already in motion to the bar as she voiced, "My handsome son paying me a visit; this calls for a celebration. Let me make you a drink. What's your fancy?"

Jake knew better than to ask for a beer. "Bourbon and water would be great," he replied, knowing that bourbon would be in supply.

"How's life in California treating you?" Karen asked as she busied herself at the bar.

"It's taking some getting used to but the weather's great," Jake replied evasively. He watched his mother and started to suspect that this would not be her first drink of the evening.

Karen came and sat down in a chair opposite Jake. There was a silence. The two never had had a chatty relationship. Karen took a long sip of her drink and said, "You look more like your dad as you get older. Funny how that happens."

Jake found the observation welcoming and saw an opening; Karen had never seemed eager to talk about Tom. "You know, Mom, I was just six when he died. Tell me something about him. Tell me what attracted you to him in the first place."

An annoyed expression, very familiar to Jake, surfaced. Already, the conversation was heading in an uncomfortable direction. She didn't like thinking about Tom because she knew she had failed him. Still, she was able to generate a superficial smile and answered, "He was a good looking guy with a good job. I thought that we could go places together."

"Did you? Did you go places?"

"We were on our way, and believe, me, Tom needed me to do it. Your dad reminded me a lot of my dad."

"In what way?"

"Nice guy, but too quick to find contentment."

"Mom, what's wrong with contentment?"

Karen was now feeling cornered by Jake's questions. She automatically hardened and responded, "Jake, I'm surprised to hear you ask that question. You're not content and you never have been. I made you that way. Contentment is for people too afraid to push ahead. You have to be tough to keep pushing and you're tough." Jake's response was nonverbal, a cynical expression on his face. Karen continued, "You don't think that I'm responsible for how you turned out? You just don't know."

"Sure Mom. I know you brought me up and all that, but aren't you willing to give me a little credit? I got myself through college with a scholarship."

"Yeah, and how did you get that scholarship?"

"From being a caddy at Burning Hills."

"How do you think you got that job?"

"Yeah, I know. You had some connections. It's not that you've never mentioned that before. But it was my idea and I applied even before you knew about it."

"But, you never would have gotten it without me; I'll tell you that. And you wouldn't have even been out looking for a job if I didn't put a fire under you."

"How did you do that, Mom?" Jake asked with more than a tinge of sarcasm.

"By not giving you anything that you wanted. You wanted something, you were going to go out and earn the money for it. Do you think the other kids you went to school with had to do that?"

"Some did."

"But they didn't have to. You did."

"I guess I'm supposed to say, 'Thanks Mom, for never giving me anything.'"

"You're damn right. And let's get this straight. I gave you plenty. You just didn't know it. I made you tough."

"I get the idea."

"I don't think you really do. I worked on this from the time you were born and I doubled my efforts after your dad died."

"Thanks, Mom," Jake replied with more sarcasm.

"You're being a smart ass, but you don't know. You were too young to remember this, but when your dad died and the funeral services were over, your Uncle Frank was there and he managed to make a fool of you and himself."

"What happened?"

"I'm not going to go into it."

"Mom, you've gone this far. You better goddamn tell me."

"Jake, since when do you think that you can tell me what to do? That's never worked for you and I can tell you this, it never will." A self-satisfying smirk crossed Karen's face, and she continued, "But, I will tell you what your sissy uncle did and then you'll see why I told him, in no uncertain terms, that he was never to have any contact with you. When I told you that your dad was dead, when you saw him laid out at the funeral home, when you saw the casket being lowered into the ground, you held yourself together as you were expected. And then at the very end, Frank picks you up and he starts crying and gets you all worked up and you start bawling and everyone was embarrassed for you.

They all just walked away and I was stuck there with the two of you."

Jake had a vague memory of his uncle picking him up but as soon as it came into his consciousness, a wave of freezing anxiety came over him. Karen was still talking, "It was pathetic. I made up my mind right there and then that you were never going to cry again. I wasn't going to have a sissy son."

All those physical sensations that came upon him when the thought of therapy arose were upon him now. Karen droned on, "I made you tough. Don't you goddamn forget it."

Jake just sat there. There was a battle going on within him, between wanting to take it all in and not wanting to hear or feel any of it. The latter was winning. It always had.

Karen was on a roll. "I think it's good, Jake, that you know all of this. Do you think you'd be in a decent career if I hadn't stepped in? You'd be teaching, for God's sake, and where do you think that would have gotten you? I hammered at you until you changed your major. You've got me to thank for that."

"Yeah, thanks, Mom," Jake replied with derision.

"You're a goddamn ingrate, that's what you are."

Jake got up and walked to the window, looking out into the darkness. He thought about his life with Maddy and Emily and realized how different it had been compared to the life he had known with his mom. He turned and looked about the room and noticed that there was no trace that Karen ever had a family, that she had a son named Jake. It suddenly occurred to him that his mom had never told him that she loved him, at least he never remembered her doing so. He turned to Karen and asked, "Mom, did you ever love me?"

Karen was taken-a-back, traumatized. Here was her big chance to simply say what she had always wanted to say, "Jake, I love you." Why couldn't she finally break through the barrier?

Jake just kept looking at her. Finally, Karen, turning her eyes away from her son, quietly uttered, "What kind of question is that for a grown man to ask?"

Jake felt like a little boy alone in the world. He had felt this feeling before. Oh, he didn't want to feel it. It was killing him. Walking toward the door, he said, "I have a plane to catch," and then he was gone.

Karen remained in her chair. Her only child had just walked out on her, this time, most likely for good. She willed her body to go rigid in an effort not to feel anything. In many ways, she had arranged her life not to feel anything. Included was the choice to not have pictures of Jake or Tom in view because the feelings they evoked were too painful. They'd be all the more painful now.

She looked across the corner window and there was a naked man getting something out of the refrigerator. This wasn't anything new; he and his wife often walked around their apartment nude. What was interesting was the way that

Karen interpreted it. Others might assume that this couple felt like they were invisible in their high-rise apartment. For Karen, it was just the opposite. It made her feel like she was the one, invisible. Like no one could see her. Like she wasn't there. After all these years, she was seventeen miles north of Beverly and forty-one floors up in the air, and she still didn't matter.

For a second, Karen almost wanted to feel something. The moment soon passed and she got up to freshen her drink.

Chapter 11: Encounter

Jake was having a hard time catching his breath. He thought that it was the elevator that was making him claustrophobic, but the situation didn't improve once he got out of the building and into the fresh air. The devils of his childhood, which had been unleashed the day that Maddy left him, were now in their full glory. The breeze off the lake had become a wind and was now spitting a light rain. Jake welcomed the striking drops against his face as a sign of life coming from the outside world, because internally, he felt that he had been annihilated. Yet he knew he was alive because he was feeling tremendous pain.

He pulled himself together enough to realize that he had to catch the L to O'Hare. If he could get there early enough, there would be time for a beer or two before boarding. He headed west to Lake and Dearborn and waited for the Blue Line. Once on the train and after it had started moving, Jake tried to distract himself by looking into the windows of the shabby apartments just a few yards from the tracks. Everything looked lonely: a naked light bulb burning in a dim hallway, a flash of a hunched over old man shuffling away from the kitchen window, a broken Big Wheel tossed on top of a rain-soaked upholstered chair in the corner of a third-story porch. These images voiced more than loneliness; they had a cry of abandonment. Rather than offering a distraction for Jake, they only intensified his throbbing pain. "What the fuck were you thinking, Uncle Frank? Why are you putting me through this?"

Jake arrived at O'Hare and took the interminable hike to his concourse. And once through security, he found his way to the bar. The bartender was an attractive redhead. She was friendly by nature, but she knew her business well enough to read that this was a customer who wanted his drink served without conversation. Jake threw down two beers before boarding.

Jake had an aisle seat over the wing. Fortunately, no one appeared to sit in the window seat next to him; it looked like the only empty seat on the plane. Across the aisle were two middle-aged women who looked like they could be sisters. As soon as was possible, Jake ordered another beer. His plan was to get drunk enough so that he could fall asleep and escape the thoughts running through his head. A parade of memories was fighting for his attention, but in a way, they were all the same, views of himself as a child all alone.

After a second beer on the plane, Jake fell into a restless sleep. The images continued in a dream state and he found himself as a little boy again. He was sitting in a dark field with the cold earth beneath him chilling his small frame. He was worried that no one would be able to find him there. Then a worse thought permeated him: not only would they not find him, no one was even looking. With that he awoke with a terrified jolt. The lady across the aisle took notice but remained silent.

With the claustrophobic feeling revisiting, Jake made a concerted effort to calm himself by taking deep breaths. The immediate sense of panic passed after a few minutes. But as he quieted himself, he started hearing a voice, his own voice as a child, asking, "Who's going to take care of me?" Jake tried to get it out of his head but it kept ruminating back, asking the same question.

Once again, Jake fell into an uneasy sleep and once again, images of loneliness marched before him, only now he saw himself as a young adult. Eventually, he found himself in that same dark field he had been in during his earlier dream. This time, he started running, running with no apparent destination other than to escape the menacing darkness. Suddenly, he eyed a small piece of granite. He realized that it was a little tombstone, but he was going at such a speed that he could not avoid tripping and flying into an abyss. Just as he realized he was in a recently dug grave, he awoke again, this time with sweat broken out on his face. His gasp for air was audible, and this time, the woman across the aisle said, "Excuse me, but are you okay?"

"Yeah, I fell asleep and had a nightmare, that's all. Thanks for asking," Jake responded in as calm a voice as possible, his effort at a smile unconvincing.

For the rest of the flight, Jake made an effort not to go to sleep; his dreams had proved more devastating than his waking thoughts. The little boy voice came back into his head. "Who's going to take care of me?" "Goddamn," Jake said to himself, wanting to run up and down the aisle and scream, "Get out of my head and leave me alone."

Finally, he could see the lights of L.A., but he knew from experience that it could take another 30 minutes before they were on the ground. Upon landing, the woman across the aisle made no effort to get out of her seat, displaying a tacit understanding of Jake's urgency to deplane.

"Good luck," she said to him.

"Thanks."

Jake raced through the airport to the parking garage and drove away quickly toward the 405. He had rolled down the window, and this time, the fresh air did help him catch his breath. With the time change, it was still the same day, 11:30

P.M. Since he had become reacquainted with his uncle, every time that he was in a crisis, he found himself drawn toward him like a magnet. Tonight was no exception. In spite of the hour, as he neared the Santa Monica exit off the 405, he turned west toward the hospital.

The hospital seemed eerily quiet except for maintenance people cleaning the floors. Jake attempted to go straight to Frank's room, but was stopped by an inquisitive nurse. "Can I help you?" she asked in a tone that was really asking, "What do you think you're doing here?"

"I'm Jake Ford. I was just passing by and thought that I'd drop by and see my Uncle Frank, Frank Ford, for a moment."

"I'm afraid that wouldn't be a good idea. He's fighting an infection and needs to be resting now."

"Oh, okay. I'll come back tomorrow," Jake replied, his own demons being supplanted by a sincere concern for his uncle.

"You might want to call first and check. Do you have the number to the nursing station?"

"Yes."

Jake returned to his car and started driving toward the Valley. He had just gotten over the hill when his cell-phone starting ringing. He didn't recognize the number.

"Hello."

"Jake, this is Frank. The nurse told me that you were just here. If you still want to visit, turn around and come right back here."

"Probably not a good idea, Uncle Frank. You need your rest."

"Let me decide that. I have a feeling that there was an important reason why you showed up at this hour and I'm not going to rest until I know what it is."

"It wasn't any big deal."

"Jake, you're not very convincing. Get over here."

"Are you sure?"

"Yes, I'm sure. And, don't worry about the nurse. I've already handled that situation."

Jake returned and as he walked by the nurse's station, the nurse who had acted as a sentinel gave him a disapproving look but said nothing. He knew the routine. He washed his hands with the sanitizer and donned a paper gown and mask before entering the room.

Frank was wide-awake and waiting for him. "Jake, I'm so relieved you came back. I mean it; I wouldn't have been able to get back to sleep if you hadn't."

Jake looked at his uncle. His welcoming smile could not disguise the deteriorating weakness of his body. He felt that he couldn't burden him with his Chicago trauma. "Uncle Frank, it really wasn't any big deal. I was just driving by."

"First of all, Jake. Take that damn mask off. I want to see your face as you talk. And, I'm not buying it. What's going on? I'll get it out of you one way or the other."

With a burst of relief, Jake simply replied. "I just came back from Chicago."

"My God, Jake, I'm so proud of you."

"I don't know what it means, Uncle Frank. All I know is that I feel…I don't know what I feel…"

"But that it's everything that you've never wanted to feel? Something like that?"

"Yeah."

"It's so scary that it feels something like death might feel?"

"Yeah, it is. And, I can't stand feeling this way. I can't. That's why I had to come see you tonight."

"I'm glad you did, Jake. Really glad. I know you've been to see Karen. Tell me what happened. Try not to leave anything out."

Jake relayed the encounter as fully as he could without going into the cemetery incident; he didn't want Frank to feel implicated. It didn't work. Frank asked, "Nothing about when your dad died, Jake? Nothing about the cemetery?"

"Goddamn it, Uncle Frank. How did you know?"

"I was there, Jake."

Jake repeated his mother's conversation about how she had been embarrassed by his crying, how she was going to make him tough, and how she was determined that he'd never cry again.

Frank chimed in, "I rode back in the limousine to your house after the cemetery. Once we got into the door, your mom gave me hell for getting you all worked up."

After a brief pause, Jake continued, "And she told you that you were to never see me again."

"She told you that, did she? Well, she probably didn't tell you all of it. After she sent you upstairs to change your clothes, she threatened to get a restraining order against me if I ever tried to come back into your life. She knew that I was a homosexual and she threatened to claim that I was preying on you. The really sick part is that twenty-three years ago, they would have believed her. At least at the time I was convinced that they would. She insisted that I leave before you came back down."

Jake got up and started pacing in what little space there is to pace in a hospital room. He decided to tell Frank about the nightmares he had on the plane, as much of it as he could stand to tell. Then a still moment passed, and Frank noticed the blood draining from Jake's face. He asked, "What's going on Jake? What are you thinking?"

"Something's coming back to me."

"Tell me what it is."

"It was that same day and I came downstairs and you were gone. I was already miserable and your leaving without saying goodbye tore me up. I started crying again. Mom told me to stop and I wouldn't. After a few minutes, she grabbed me by the hand and pulled me down the basement stairs…. I don't want to think about this anymore."

"Jake, you've got to. Tell me what happened in the basement."

Jake paced for a few seconds and continued, "She led me into the fruit cellar and said, 'This is what you get for all your crying today. I'm going to make you tough. You're going to stay down here until I'm good and ready to let you out, and if I hear you crying, I'm never going to open this door.' Then she closed the door."

"Oh my God, Jake! How long did she leave you there?"

"I don't know but I remember that it was totally dark. There was a light you could turn on by pulling a string but I was too short to reach it. I remember feeling real panicky because if mom didn't come and get me, there would be no one else looking for me. After a while, I got tired from standing and sat down on the floor. That floor was earthen and I remember how cold it was. I think I fell asleep. I don't have any memory of her coming down and letting me out."

"Jake, my poor boy Jake. I should have never left you there."

"There wasn't much you could do about it, was there?" Jake asked, his voice still full of anxiety and his body still in motion.

"Not really." Frank was quiet while he gathered his thoughts and then resumed, "but I think I can help you now." Jake continued his pacing. "Jake, I can explain what all this means in your life, now."

Frustration showed on Jake's face. "Uncle Frank, after all that's happened tonight, I don't think that I can stand to hear anymore."

"But Jake, that's exactly the point. It's already on the surface; now's the time to take away its power." Jake's anxious expression didn't change but he continued to listen. "Take those dreams, for instance. I think they tell the whole story. Let's go back to the day of the funeral. You had seen your father being lowered into the ground and you knew that he had left you for good. You felt abandoned by him as any six-year-old would.

"Then when you came home, the one parent you still had left put you in the basement and let you know that she had the power to leave you down there. You sat on the ground and got chilled, and it reminded you of the cemetery; you had just seen your dad lowered into the cold ground a few hours earlier. You said that you fell asleep. You probably dreamed that you had been abandoned by both of your parents and essentially left for dead in the cemetery. Remember telling me in the first dream that you felt that no one could find you, but then you really panicked when you realized that no one was looking?"

"Yeah," Jake replied, "but I didn't know that I was in a cemetery in that first dream."

Frank continued in an emphatic voice, "Doesn't make any difference. In your six-year-old mind, the cellar earth and the cemetery became one and the same thing. And, besides, by the second dream, you had figured it out. In the first dream you were a child, in the second, an adult. In your adult sub-conscious, you had made the connection; you knew you were in the cemetery."

"Uncle Frank, I think I need to go."

"Jake, wait just a minute. Let's connect the dots from then until now. Think about it. You were told that if you ever cried, you were essentially going to be left for dead. As a kid, you had to believe that. What choice did you have in the matter? Let me ask you this. Do you remember ever crying since that day?"

202

"No."

"Jake, it all comes together. You were told that to be in touch with your feelings was the same as a death warrant. You believed it, totally. You grew up, became an adult, and yet that lock remains in place. Don't you remember the night that you told me that Maddy was insisting that you go to counseling? I asked you why you wouldn't do it and you said, 'It would goddamn kill me?'"

"And it is goddamn killing me," Jake replied in a pressured voice. "Uncle Frank, I can't take this anymore. All this may be connecting the dots for you but it's killing me. This isn't one of your books where you pull everything together at the end so that it all falls in place. This is me, and everything coming together isn't helping. I feel… I can't describe it but it's so intense that I don't think I can stand it much longer. I've got to get out of here."

"Jake, don't leave this way."

"I've gotta. I can't stand being in this room any longer. I can't stand being trapped in my body any longer." With that, Jake rushed out of the room and into the early morning darkness.

That evening, Michael arrived at his club. For a couple of weeks now, he had been playing with a new opponent, Jake. Michael was the constant victor but Jake held his own, and in time, with Michael's instruction, and Jake's advantage of youth, that could change.

Michael had something else on his mind. Dr. Steiner had called, telling him that Frank's immune system was now so compromised that they wouldn't be able to continue chemotherapy unless Frank could undergo a successful bone marrow transplant. Time was closing in and Michael knew the odds of finding a good match were dismal. If Frank had living parents or brothers or sisters, there would be a 30 to 40 percent chance. But, he didn't. Jake was too far removed to even be under consideration. They'd have to investigate a national registry but hope there was remote.

At first Michael thought that Jake was running late; that was always a possibility with Southern California traffic. After an hour, Michael tried Jake's cell phone and then he tried Frank's house. No answer at either number. He still had Jake's business card in his wallet and called the station. Jake hadn't been in all day.

Chapter 12: Released

Michael awoke the next morning and raised the blind from his bedroom window. Beneath him, waves from the Pacific lazily sauntered upon the beach, only to rhythmically retreat. When he had first moved into his condo, he had been struck by the coincidence that he had grown up on Pacific Avenue in Pittsburgh and now could see its namesake from his windows.

Michael's upbringing had been comfortable. His dad was a produce wholesaler and provided a good living for his wife and three sons. Michael had been the youngest. As far as accepting his sexuality, his experience had been quite different than Frank's. Michael recognized that he was attracted to males and simply accepted it for what it was. It didn't deter him from his military career or any other pursuit. He had been content with his love life without ever really falling in love. Until he met Frank.

After Jake's no-show at the health club, Michael worked out with weights and then stopped by St. John's to see Frank. As he entered the room, a visibly anxious Frank said, "I'm really worried about Jake," and then unloaded the drama of the previous night.

"I don't think I ever told you, and Jake doesn't remember this, but when he was a child, he used to call me Uncle Wonderful. He doesn't think I'm so wonderful now." A few seconds of silence fell and Frank repeated, "I'm really worried about him."

 "I'm sure he's okay," Michael offered assuredly. He didn't share with Frank the fact that Jake had just stood him up at the health club. "He's not the kind of guy that would do anything rash. He's tough."

"Don't use that word. His mother committed all kinds of crimes against that boy in the name of making him tough."

"I'll track him down, Frank. You have to stop worrying about him. This kind of stress is harmful to you right now."

Michael changed the subject and asked, "Did you see Dr. Steiner today?" knowing that he had.

"Yes, she was here."

"And, did she discuss the bone marrow transplant?" Michael asked, not wanting to pussyfoot around such an urgent subject.

"Yes, she did. But, Michael, in spite of her optimism, both you and I know the chances of finding a match are practically nil. Let's face reality."

"I'll tell you one reality. As long as there's any chance of your recovering, your ability to think positive and eliminate as much stress as possible is key. For the time being, you have to let me do your worrying for you. As for Jake, you may not like the word, "tough", but he is. He's okay. You'll see soon enough."

"Not soon enough for me."

"Remember, I'm doing the worrying for now," Michael replied with as reassuring of a smile he could muster.

But, it was now the next morning and Michael had called Jake's cell phone and Frank's house and there was no answer. He called KLF and was told for a second time, "he's not in today." Michael was worried.

Late afternoon of that same day, Frank was tossing restlessly when an attractive young blonde entered his room. She said, "Hello, Mr. Ford, I'm Maddy."

Frank smiled. "Of course, I know who you are. I know Emily, remember? You couldn't be anyone other than you; she looks so much like you. Take off that damn mask so I can really see you."

"I will for a second," she replied in compliance. She continued, "Mr. Ford, Jake's okay. He asked me to come here and tell you."

"Oh, thank God!" Frank cried out. "I've been so worried about him. I was afraid that I pushed him over the edge. Deep down, I knew he wouldn't harm himself, but still..." his voice trailed off.

"He's okay. He's at home, home in Studio City, trying to get some sleep." Frank's face brightened as Maddy continued, "He's home to stay, Mr. Ford."

"No news could make me happier," Frank replied in total honesty. Jake's life coming together meant more to him than his own at this point. He continued, "And, quit calling me Mr. Ford. Call me Uncle Frank. Now, tell me what happened."

"I was walking toward the cafeteria during my noon break and, as I passed through the atrium, I saw Jake waiting for me; he pretty much knows my patterns. He looked like a zombie; I could tell he hadn't slept for a few days. He came up to me and asked if we could take a walk outside. Once we were in the big rose garden, and no one was around us, he poured his heart out. He told me all about his trip to Chicago, about his mother, about when his dad had died, about his horrible nightmares and about how he hadn't been able to sleep since. He said that if it means that he has to go into therapy to, in his words, 'shake off all this shit,' then he was ready to do it. Immediately, I told him that I'd help him in any way I could. We talked for about a half hour and then I suggested that he'd probably be able to sleep better if he were in our bed. Uncle Frank, to see how much tension left his face when I told him that, was both heart wrenching and beautiful." Maddy paused for a moment before adding in a quiet voice, "My beautiful Jake."

There were tears on Frank's face as Maddy continued, "Uncle Frank, you'll never know how grateful I am to you. You showed him the way home." They both sat quietly for a few moments. Then Maddy said, "I hate to rush off, I've waited so long to meet you, but I have to pick up Emily from school. She'll be so happy her daddy's home." As she walked toward the door, she interjected, "Oh, Jake asked me to call your friend, Michael. He knows that I was on my way here."

Frank fell asleep. Michael's visit later that day was brief, knowing that a good solid sleep was the best thing possible to replenish Frank's resources. And sleep he did, fairly constantly into the following afternoon.

By the time he was fully awake, he had another visitor. It was Jake. He still looked beat-up but he flashed his patented smile as he said, "Hi, Uncle Frank. How are you doing?"

Frank smiled back, "How are you doing? That's the more interesting question."

"To be honest, Uncle Frank, I feel like I've been to hell and back since I was in this room a couple of days ago."

"I'm glad you made it back," Frank replied, again with a smile. Tell me about it. Tell me where you were for those couple days."

"When I left here, I didn't know where I was going. Seems like I've been doing that a lot lately. Anyway, I got this crazy idea that I'd drive down to Mexico. I haven't been across the border yet. When I got to San Diego, I was feeling too trapped in the car so I decided to stop there and I found my way to Mission Beach. I left my cell phone in the consul...I knew I didn't want to talk with anyone...I knew I couldn't. I got out and just started walking. Even though I was so tired, I was also so wired that I knew I couldn't sleep and walking seemed to help.

About 8:00 in the morning, I called KLF and told them that I wouldn't be in for the rest of the week, that some family matter had come up. I found a motel and got a room. Still couldn't sleep. I tried watching TV. Ever watch daytime television? That made me more anxious. So, I returned to the beach and walked. I lost track of time but, eventually it got dark. I knew I should eat but my whole body was just so tense that it would be too hard to swallow. All the while, everything that had come up the night before kept passing through my mind. Worse than that,

I kept feeling everything I had felt. Finally, I went back to my room and tried sleeping, but every few minutes I kept leaping out of bed like a spring, too tense to stay put. As soon as it was daylight, I got up and checked out.

"I was driving back to L.A. and as I was passing the exit for Sunrise Beach, I found myself heading in that direction. Uncle Frank, it was like I was being pulled toward your special place. When I got there, except for some early morning surfers, I had the beach to myself. I climbed over the rocks and made it to the cove. The sky was overcast and, compared to the day we were there, the waves crashing against the rocks were more turbulent and the spray coming up on my face, more forceful.

I sat down where we had sat, and for the first time in two days, was able to sit still. It was as if the spray was calming me down. I sat there and I thought of you being with me, and after a while, I laid back, I put my sweater under my head, and fell asleep, I think for a couple of hours. When I woke up, I knew what I had to do; that spray had knocked some sense into me.

I had to stop running. I had to deal with the shit. Once I accepted that, I looked at my watch and realized that I could find Maddy over her lunchbreak. You know the rest."

"Jake, I keep saying this, but I'm so proud of you. You have the courage to stare down your demons and you're going to win; the worst is over."

"I sure hope so."

"Jake, remember during one of our early visits, I was talking about how allowing oneself to feel vulnerable is how you get at the real problems? And getting at the real problems is how you solve them? I knew you didn't like hearing that."

"I didn't, that's for sure."

"Well, you've done it, just the same."

Jake's visit was brief but before he left, he shared with Frank his decision to return to school and prepare himself to teach. He'd have to work and study at the same time, but he didn't care how long it would take; he was going to do it. Maddy was behind him 100%.

The following day, a biopsy in Frank's pelvic area was performed. Then the sample would be analyzed and matched to bone marrow in the national registry. Unbeknownst to Frank, Jake called Michael and insisted that he be tested as a possible donor. Michael explained to him that children of patients are considered too distant to be a donor, never mind a nephew. Jake made such a nuisance of himself, he had called Dr. Stiener as well, that they finally arranged for Jake to be tested.

It took a few days for the results to come back. Nothing matched in the national registry, but wonder of wonders, beyond a wonder really, Jake's marrow presented a match. At least it was awfully close, and if they administered the right steroids at the right time, maybe there was a chance. It was the only chance.

Frank would have to be fully recovered from his infection before the transplant could take place.

When the infection cleared, he asked if he could go home for a few days. He felt he needed some closure that being in his own home would provide. Permission was granted to go home for a weekend prior to the transplant which would take place the following Tuesday. Michael would stay with him around the clock.

On Sunday night, Michael was standing by the bed. "Michael," Frank said in a voice obviously fatigued by his illness, "Sit down next to me; there's something I need to tell you. A few months ago, Jake was over here and was upset. And before he stormed out of the house, he yelled at me, 'You keep yourself cooped up in this house,' a museum he called it.

'What is it that you're so afraid of?'" I've had plenty of time to think about things since then and I realized that he was right, I was afraid of something." Frank stopped and looked at Michael before continuing. I was afraid that I'd be hurt again. I was too afraid to fall in love again." Frank now reached for Michael's hand. "But, the truth is, I have been in love. I've been in love with you." A deep expression crossed

Michael's face that Frank couldn't interpret. "Michael, I know that there was a time when you were in love with me, too. Had I only had the courage to love you back then."

In a tender voice Michael responded, "For a guy who thinks he can always read the situation, you haven't done a very good job with this one. Don't you know that I've never stopped being in love with you? That I love you now more than ever?"

"Really, Michael?"

Michael stood up and undressed. He crawled into bed with Frank and held his frail body in his arms. All the agitation that Frank had been feeling throughout the day, his apprehension toward the transplant, melted away. He soon fell into a comfortable sleep. A silent tear rolled down Michael's cheek. He had waited five years.

Frank went back to the hospital Monday afternoon. They wanted him rested for the transplant the following day. However, when the strict nurse, who had stopped Jake the week before, saw him walking down the hall, she just turned her head. Jake washed his hands, put on the gown and mask, and entered Frank's room. Frank wasn't really sleeping, just cruising, and he immediately knew that Jake was there.

"Hey, this is great. I didn't think broom Hilda would let anybody past her tonight. I'm supposed to be resting, as if they can command someone to do that."

"I know. Michael called and told me. Still, I didn't think it could hurt to stop in for just a moment."

"Seeing you is the best tonic I know, Jake. Particularly now, after what you've been through in the last week. It means so much to me that you wanted to come tonight."

"Uncle Frank, there's something I want to ask you."

"Sure, anything, Jake."

"It will probably sound stupid, but I want you to try real hard to pull through this thing. I want you to do everything you can do to stick around awhile."

"Jake, that's the nicest thing anyone ever asked me to do. My son, (the first time Frank ever used this expression with Jake), I'll do my best; I'll give it 110% because you asked me to."

Relief emanated from Jake's face. "Good." That's all he said. He wanted to squeeze his uncle's hand but knew he would be violating isolation procedures. Instead, he gave his trademark smile and left the room.

On Tuesday, the transplant took place. Jake had been given a local anesthetic while the marrow was being harvested from his pelvic area. Meanwhile, Frank had been treated with high doses of anti-cancer drugs before he would receive the bone marrow through a central venous catheter.

It would take two weeks before knowing if Jake's human leukocyte-associated antigens matched in sufficient number to be accepted by Frank's antigens. That wait did not deter Frank's immediate high spirits. Not only had Jake presented him with a new opportunity to be cured, but he was also feeling the euphoria of being in love with Michael and knowing that he was loved back. What a difference a week could make.

On day ten, the situation became worrisome. Signs of host rejection were becoming apparent and increased steroids were being administered. The consulting transplant physician had called in Dr. Steiner, who in turn, had called Michael. The additional treatment did not halt the downhill slide, and, a few hours later, Michael notified Jake and Maddy.

An anxiety-ridden Jake, along with Maddy, entered the room. Jake looked toward Michael for reassurance but found none. Then, signs of stabilization occurred and Michael, Jake, and Maddy, all shared renewed hope. Other doctors came and went but most of the time now, it was the three of them who remained with Frank.

At 9:15 p.m., Frank slipped into a coma and by 10:00, the heart monitor indicated that Frank was slipping away. Jake, reading the faces of those who could interpret the monitor, cried out, "Uncle Frank, you're not going to die. You can't. You're going to turn this thing around. Everything will be okay. Remember, we talked about it? You said you'd give 110%! Remember?"

Maddy started to cry softly and Jake took her in his arms and held her tight. The soft heaving of her chest brought back to Jake that day in the cemetery when he was six and Frank had held him. He had felt Frank's chest heave as well, and that had given him permission to cry. Jake started to cry now. For the first time since he was six, he cried. He cried for his dad, he cried for the desperate loneliness of his childhood, and now, he was crying because he was losing his Uncle Frank. Maddy held him several minutes as he sobbed. Then with her eye on the heart monitor, she said, "Jake, Uncle Frank is slipping into ventricular fibrillation. It will only be a few minutes more."

Jake grabbed his uncle's hand and among the sobs, said, "Uncle Frank, I love you. Thank you, Uncle Frank. Thank you for everything." He started sobbing louder again and then he got down and put his uncle's hand against his tear-soaked cheek. "And, oh, one more thing," he uttered between sobs, "I always knew that you were my Uncle Wonderful."

A minute later, Michael, who had been holding Frank's other hand, bent down and kissed him on the forehead.

Epilogue:

Frank had written a letter and left it with Michael in case the transplant had been unsuccessful. It read:

Dear Jake,

You know me; there's always a few more things I want to tell you. I asked myself: if I were to leave you with one piece of advice, what would it be? I thought it over and decided it would be this: "In order to find yourself, you have to give yourself away." That concept has been the saving grace of my life. But then I thought about it more and realized you already understood this. You literally insisted that a part of you become a part of me. I also realized that you understood this when I thought about your desire to teach. Teaching is all about giving yourself to others.

There's a family story I wanted to tell you that I never got around to. Remember those antique oak chairs that I told you had belonged to my maternal grandmother? I think I told you about Grandfather and his drinking problem, but I never told you about Grandmother. She immigrated from Ireland with less than an 8th grade education, but she was smart enough about money that she owned several pieces of real estate before she died.

I tell you this now because you'll soon find out that, with the exception of a few personal items I am leaving to Michael, you are my only heir. I turned out to be pretty smart about money, too. When I had that job as a night auditor in the brokerage house in New York, I started studying trades of the really successful brokers and started noticing patterns and trends. I followed suit. As a writer, I never knew how long my career would last so I was careful over the years to hang onto what I had earned. It became a way of life. That brings me back to your education. I hope you take some of this money and go back to school full time. No sense making it hard on yourself.

Now, Jake, something personal. I may have been out of your life for twenty-three years, but I always knew where you were. I had friends in Chicago who kept me informed. I knew the day you married and I knew when you had moved to California.

I wasn't able to be part of your life during your growing up years, so thank you for making the effort to come back into mine. Even though our reunion has been brief, it changed my life and made it richer and happier than you'll ever know.

I love you very much,

Uncle Frank

(continue)

Jake never saw the letter.

The heart monitor had slipped into ventricular fibrillation but it never reached asystole, which is ventricular stand still. Frank had experienced a pseudo rejection of Jake's antigens, but his heart was so strong from his years of swimming that he had been able to withstand it. His heart rhythms reversed and by midnight he came out of his coma.

When Frank was strong enough, he set up a trust fund for Jake to go back to school. Whether Jake accepts it remains to be seen. One thing Jake will never know.

Acknowledgements

To my sister Carolyn Benner, who served as editor. To Anji Strasburger who served as copy editor. Mara Davis as proofreader. And to Todd Hipsher, who helped me with every techy aspect of writing and publishing this book.